"An Unprecedented Occasion:
the deflowering of a lower-class Dubuque Irish
ex-Catholic by a snotty Kansas City Jewish
cardboard box heiress. In a Boone motel! Do you
realize what the odds are against such a thing
ever happening? Save the registration receipt. I
can sell photostats of it by mail."

Also by Robert Byrne:

ONCE A CATHOLIC

Always A Catholic

A novel by
Robert Byrne

PINNACLE BOOKS   NEW YORK

ALWAYS A CATHOLIC

Copyright © 1981 by Robert Byrne

An original Pinnacle Books edition, published for the first time anywhere.

First printing, October 1981

ISBN: 0-523-41166-9

Cover illustration by John Solie

Printed in the United States of America

PINNACLE BOOKS, INC.
1430 Broadway
New York, New York 10018

For Teressa Skelton

Contents

ALWAYS A CATHOLIC

1

A Change of Life

We were sitting in the depot, my parents and I, waiting for the bus that would take me to Iowa State. It wasn't easy. The problem was that my mother was using the occasion as a springboard into deep grief. I was leaving home for the first time, and we would be separated by a hundred and eighty miles of unfamiliar cornfields. Why, she wanted to know, couldn't I spend a third year at highly-regarded Crown of Thorns College right there in Dubuque? She had tagged each piece of my luggage, including the shopping bag and the cardboard box, with numbers for people to call in case I was overwhelmed by catastrophe, and she had pinned an emergency ten-dollar bill to my shorts. In a repeat performance she burst into tears, threw her arms around me, gave me advice better suited to an infant than a fully-mature twenty-year-old, and scorned my father's efforts to lighten the mood.

I wasn't the only person in the world with a problem that fine September morning in 1950. Waves of opium-crazed Communists, for example, were pouring south across Korea's 38th Parallel, sending the defenders of freedom reeling backward toward the port city of Pusan. The way my mother was acting, you would have thought I was headed for Pyongyang rather than Ames.

"Would you calm down, Mom, and stop worrying?" I

1

said in a strained whisper, glancing around the waiting room. "People are staring."

"What kind of a mother would I be if I didn't worry?"

People couldn't help staring, for when it came to expressing grief and worry my gray-haired mother was a virtuoso of awesome gifts. The lines in her face, which she could multiply and deepen at will, radiated agony. Her posture suggested not only that she was carrying a crushing spiritual load, but that she would go on carrying it until it killed her. At funerals she presented such a heart-wrenching figure of despair that even undertakers were known to sniffle a little. Next to her the family of the deceased looked like cheerleaders.

"I'm only going away to school, Mom," I said, "just like thousands of other kids. They all get plenty of sleep and plenty to eat and they keep warm and dry."

She clutched my arm as if to keep me from capsizing. "The Stoody boy went away to school," she said, "and within three weeks he was run over by a train."

"That was in 1932," my father said with a wave of his hand. "Tommy will be all right, Margaret! He's smart! He's tough! A Shannon if ever there was one."

"They've started another war," she said. "Next they'll want my baby for that."

I was the baby in question. Tall. Lean. Hard. Pimpled. There was no immediate danger of my getting drafted. The government was operating on the assumption that smart people were better than dumb people and that brains were vital to the strength of the free world. Since brains worked perfunctorily if at all when ventilated by bullet holes, it was folly to expose them to gunfire. Students who did well on tests, therefore, were exempt from the draft. All I had to do to avoid getting drawn into an Asian land war was keep my grades up, which I explained to my mother without effect while wishing the bus would come. She said there was no reason I couldn't live at home and continue at Crown of Thorns, which was as fine an institution of higher learning as there was anywhere in the world. I agreed that Crown of Thorns was one heck of an institution of higher learning, especially for people interested in careers in Latin and choral music. What the school was weak on was sanitary engineering, which had been chosen

2

as my life's work by my father. By contrast, Iowa State had an absolutely stunning school of sanitary engineering, so that's where I was going.

My father had faith in the future of sewage and in my ability to handle the technical courses required in learning to cope with it professionally. I had been good at math right from the time the nuns first sprang it on me at St. Procopius. The secret of my success at math, I think, was that I never minded letting *x* equal the unknown. Other kids never seemed to want to do it. The very idea made them sweat. Whenever the teacher talked about the unknown and letting it equal *x*, they thought about running away from home. I liked a subject in which unknowns were acknowledged instead of swept under the rug. They could call them *x* or anything else as far as I was concerned. What intrigued me was that unknowns could be manipulated and used. Sometimes they could be canceled out of equations entirely, leaving an answer that seemed unattainable at the beginning. Far from being hostile to *x*, I welcomed it. For my money there were a lot of things in life that people pretended to know all about that would have been better off being allowed to equal *x*.

"Oh, I don't know," Mom said with a graveside sigh. "I hope this whole thing isn't a mistake."

"It's no mistake," Dad said. "It's time the boy was out on his own. He's got a fine mind and he'll get good grades. Two years from now he'll be an outstanding sanitary engineer and never have to worry about a job."

"So far from home," Mom said. She wanted me to be a floorwalker at Monkey Ward's so she could fix me a hot lunch for the rest of my life. "And the money," she added. "The money alone is reason enough."

"Let me worry about the money," Dad said. "Sending him to college is the best investment I'll ever make. You'll pay us back, won't you, Tommy?"

"You're darned right, Dad. I'll keep track of every penny." I meant it, too. I knew what a sacrifice they were making for me.

"It's money in the bank," Dad said, warming to the subject. "You take Karl Balzer. When he took over the Dubuque treatment plant five years ago he was making six hundred a month. Now he's pulling down eight hundred.

3

What does he do for it? Reads a few dials and chews the fat with his secretary. He's not on his feet all day wondering where the next customer is coming from, like I am." My father had gone back to barbering after the failure of his construction business. "No, sir. His customers can't help themselves. They've *got* to send them their business. What else can they do, eh? That's the kind of line to be in. No competition. Nobody's going to open a *rival* treatment plant."

He spoke partly to me and my mother and partly to a family nearby, who stared at him with open fascination. My mother, having heard the speech before, sank to a bench and started a rosary. Her lips flickered and the beads dripped from her fist like water from a faucet. She could speed through ten Hail Marys without inhaling, pronouncing each one as if it was a single world fifty-three syllables long. She was a Hail Mary machine.

"Where there are people, there is bound to be sewage," Dad went on enthusiastically. "And where there is sewage, there's got to be treatment, because otherwise people would drop like flies. Population is going up every year, and so is Karl Balzer's salary. His game is sewage, and he'll never have to worry about running short of it. I'll tell you another thing: He's one of the most respected men in the Knights of Columbus."

"His color is poor," Mom said. "He's going to die soon."

"For God's sake!"

"Dad, I know you're against it, but maybe I should look around for a part-time job at school. I could earn enough to—"

"No! Money is my department. You worry about your grades. To interest a top-notch treatment plant you've got to get top-notch grades. Get lousy grades and you'll end up in a city dump somewhere directing garbage trucks, up to your knees in orange peels and lettuce."

"Oh, say, Tommy," Mom said, perking up. "I packed you a lunch. It's in the gray grip, wrapped in the rain coat. It'll be nice to have a bite along about Marshalltown."

"Thanks, Mom."

The westbound bus groaned to a stop at the curb alongside the building, setting off a flurry of handshaking and

4

hugging in the waiting room. The bus driver stepped to the curb and shouted, "Fillmore, Langworthy, Cedar Rapids, Ames, Des Moines, Guthrie Center, Wiota, Fiscus, and Omaha." He threw open a door on the side of the bus and began throwing bags inside. I had to run to rescue the suitcase with my lunch in it.

"Don't forget the sacraments," Mom reminded me before I got on. "Go see Father Slattery first thing. He knows you're coming. He'll tell you when the Masses are and introduce you at the Newman Club." Father Slattery had been reassigned from Dubuque to Ames several years before.

"Be a good boy," Dad said, shaking my hand vigorously, "that's the main thing."

"It takes more than just being good," Mom said. "You have to practice the sacraments, too. We'll be praying for you. Go to church. Change your sheets."

"I didn't mean *only* be good," Dad said with a trace of irritation. "Naturally there is more to it than that."

"Tell him how important his religion is, Leonard. It should come from the father, even though he doesn't set the best example, night after night at the American Legion with that stinking, rotten Arnold Gertz."

Dad didn't react to the slurs because Mom spoke them more out of habit than intention. She denounced alcohol, the Legion, and Mr. Gertz so often that the words had became, in effect, inaudible to my father.

"Don't sell your religion short, son," Dad said. "Get your sleep."

"Don't oversleep, though," Mom said. "That's not good, either. Makes you logy all day."

"Good-bye, Mom! Good-bye, Dad! I'll write!"

"I'd be lost without my faith," Mom said, "just lost."

I tried to get on the bus, but my mother held me back. I kissed her salty cheek and looked at her face. I had never seen so much worry in one spot in all my life. Her face was like a depression into which all the worry from the surrounding countryside drained. "I hope we don't live to regret this," she said. "If something happens to you, I don't think I could go on."

I was the last one to board the bus and was talking to my

5

parents through the open door, Mom's hand tight around my wrist. The driver was behind the wheel, waiting for us to wrap it up.

"It's not as if I'm disappearing from the face of the earth, Mom," I said. "I'll be mailing you my laundry."

Dad pried loose her grip on my arm. "Hit those books!" he said. "Show them you mean business right off the bat!"

"I will. Good-bye. . . ."

"Ask God's help," Mom said.

"I will."

"Get right down on your knees and ask God to help you."

"Okay, Mom."

"It won't hurt you to get down on your knees." She pressed something lumpy into my hand and closed my fingers around it.

"Whatever happens," Dad said, "remember that you're a Shannon."

There was a hiss of air as the driver released the brakes. "I'll make sure he writes," the driver said to my mother as the door folded shut.

I found a window seat and waved. Mom was leaning against Dad for support. Her pale hands fluttered to her breast, a rosary crisscrossing them like veins. She struggled to keep her trembling lower lip from going out of control. My father, a large man with an impressive expanse of stomach and a revealingly pink nose, beamed proudly, one arm around my mother's shoulders and the other raised high, like the Statue of Liberty. I kept them in view as long as I could, and when they were out of sight my eyes clouded over with tears. A guy couldn't have asked for better parents. They were behind me a hundred percent.

In the case of my father, the percentage may have reached a hundred only a few years before. Until my voice changed he didn't spend much time with me. He didn't enjoy the company of people who giggled and fidgeted and who couldn't drink a bottle of Dubuque Star beer without passing out or throwing up. He was not fond of Porky Schornhorst, Kites Callahan, Elbows Hilken, and my other friends from the puberty years, and who could blame him? When he saw that I was moving away from the idea of tomfoolery as a career and that I was a good enough student to profit from college, he took a more active interest in my life. After giving up the construction business, which had kept him depressed and preoccupied, he became one of my most voluble supporters.

While it was true that my mother didn't have the same flair for hilarity as she did for gloom, she wasn't dreary all the time. Listening to Fibber McGee and Molly on the radio, she sometimes laughed out loud. When that happened, though, she usually applied the brakes, as if suddenly remembering that nowhere in her Sunday missal did the word *guffaw* appear. I don't think it's in the Bible, either. The Bible was one of the few books we had in the house, but it was rarely opened, not even by my mother. Reading God's words raw was treacherous without professional help, a fact easily proven by pointing at all the Protestants we have on our hands today. Holy Scripture requires *interpretation,* which is where the Church comes in. To figure out what God could possibly have had in mind in a couple of verses, you need an understanding of defunct tongues and old-world cultural flux. Who has time for that except the cloistered? There are two good synonyms for Bible study: exegesis and hermeneutics. You pick the one you want, depending on the music of the sentence.

There was nothing funny about Catholicism in its official dress. Yet, a lot of Catholics I knew were funny. The discrepancy bothered me. Why were there no saints known for their senses of humor?

It figured that Mom hated to see me climb into the bus. Two years earlier she had lost my brother Paul to a monastic order famous for the depth of its cloister. As far as the family was concerned, he was in a land of the living dead. We were supposed to be comforted by knowing how pleased God was. Paul had never been able to get himself organized after World War II, to which he contributed a foot. Just before taking his final vows, he visited home wearing a black cassock and cowl. Kites Callahan, who believed that blasphemy and sacrilege were all right if they were funny enough, saw him limping around in front of our house and called him "Hopalong Chastity." Kites was himself handicapped with a congenital defect that apparently was incurable. He had been born without a sense of propriety.

7

As the bus crossed Grandview Avenue at Ludwig's Grocery Store and headed down the hill toward Rockdale, I opened my hand to see what my mother had put there. It was her second best rosary, the one that was blessed by Henry P. Uhlman, coadjutor archbishop of Dyersville.

2

Catholic Asthma

When the bus reached the cemetery outside of town, I opened the paperback book I intended to study during the trip to the interior: *Words: Rocket Fuel for the Brain*. A sharp command of the English language, I reasoned, would make my rise to the top of the sanitary-engineering pyramid a veritable certainty. In sophomore religion at Crown of Thorns I was assigned an article on the question of God's existence by Mortimer J. Adler, one of the smartest Catholics extant. His prose was so strewn with hard words that I was barely able to catch the drift of his argument, which, if I remember correctly, was that God probably did exist. A secondary, unstated point was that smart people used hard words. I wanted to be smart; therefore I had to use them, too. Oblivious to several non sequiturs, I threw myself into *Thirty Days to a More Powerful Vocabulary*, finishing it in twenty-seven. By the time I left for Iowa State I had compiled a list of two hundred words that nobody had ever heard of and was headed for a thousand. Anyone I might meet in the academic, business, or professional worlds who resorted to sesquipedalianism as a means of obfuscation was in for a rude surprise.

But on the bus that day, I couldn't concentrate. I was on my own and my body was alive with excitement. By twisting in my seat and pressing my cheek to the window, I could gaze upon the city that had been the scene of my birth, infancy, puberty, adolescence, and incipient manhood. For the first time in my life I felt a wave of emotion that I was later to learn was nostalgia. In the foreground the green and golden farmlands sloped toward the Catfish Creek valley and my cousin Willie's barn and silo, then rose to the tree-lined fairways of the Dubuque Country Club and the homes of the rich. The elms, maples, birches, and oaks that lined the streets make the town look like a national park. Dubuque probably would have been better off had it been declared a national park. As it was, the population of forty-five thousand was too dependent on the sash and door factory, the coffin works, and the meatpacking company. The new John Deere tractor plant helped, but, I gathered from relatives, it was attracting outsiders, some of them of an inappropriate color, about which the less said in front of the children the better. From the high ground near the cemetery I could see all the way to Mount Sinsinawa in Wisconsin and the blue hills of Illinois, both on the other side of the Mississippi. In all directions the landscape was lush and rolling and picturesque and beautiful. The chamber of commerce called the area "the Switzerland of America," a comparison that didn't seem farfetched to those of us who had never been in Europe. Despite the beauty, tourism was not making a major impact on Dubuque. Julien Dubuque's grave was interesting, Eagle Point Park was one of the jewels of the Work Projects Administration, and nearby Galena boasted a house once lived in by Useless S. Grant. Nevertheless, no significant number of tourists was being diverted from Niagara Falls and the Grand Canyon. A lack of publicity was the reason, according to my father.

The bus followed Highway 151 around a left-hand curve on the way to Cascade, cutting off my line of sight. By kneeling on the back seat I was able to keep the environs whence I had sprung in view a little longer. At the far right were the slate roofs of the Mount Carmel nunnery, where I had once stumbled across a gaggle of postulants in flying white habits playing volleyball. Why it was so jarring to see a display of physical joy from nuns, even nascent nuns, I don't know, for I was already old enough at the time to know that nuns had once been people.

In the center of the horizon was the squared-off brick

steeple of St. Procopius Church. It had originally been topped by a tall wooden cone with a cross on top, but shortly after its completion in 1923 God inadvertently destroyed it with a lightning bolt. In high school I tried to find out who St. Procopius was. Aside from the fact that he was the patron saint of acne, little was known. An unfounded rumor held that he was the one who drove the snakes *into* Ireland so that St. Patrick could drive them out. Somebody had to do it.

At the left in the far distance I could barely see the steeple of the Chapel of Christ the Conqueror on the Crown of Thorns campus. Aside from the radio transmitter, it was the tallest structure in the tristate area and was designed to show the Protestants once and for all who was boss. The Protestants didn't have a steeple for miles that even began to compare with it. Next to the chapel, on a block of native limestone, was a larger-than-life statue of the college's founder, Bishop Duncan MacSwain, his hand raised to his face in a blessing. If you stood below and to the side of the monument, you could match the Bishop's thumb to the tip of his nose. Brambles had been planted to discourage cameramen from seeking the proper angle. In the middle of the last century, the then Monsignor MacSwain stood on top of the hill now climbed by Fourteenth Street and blessed the fast-growing community below him, protecting it forever from property damage due to tornadoes. He mentioned tornadoes specifically, they say, though why he singled them out is a mystery. It was a costly choice. If he had banned floods instead, Dubuque would be millions of dollars ahead. Anyone genuinely concerned about property damage would certainly have zeroed in on floods, for the Mississippi surged out of its banks almost every spring. A meteorology student once told me that the ruggedness of the local terrain made tornadoes impossible, but he came from a strong Methodist family. Catholics felt that the blessing had been miraculously successful, and talk was heard about an eventual sainthood for Bishop MacSwain. Had the Roman Curia gone so far as to send a delegate to look into the idea, he would have soon found himself in a theological thicket; winds *similar* to tornadoes from time to time ripped roofs off on the *edges* of the town. The problem would be to define precisely such concepts as *tornado*

11

and *Dubuque*. A great deal of expense and debate would be avoided if those who bestowed blessings used more specific language. Ideally they should draw up a document like an insurance policy so that everyone concerned would know what was covered and what was excluded.

When my past was no longer in view, I left the rear window, returned to my seat, and faced my future. Iowa State was rushing toward me like an unknown planet. I felt an uneasiness that must also have troubled my mother: On the campus of a godless state college the fortress of my faith would come under heavy attack. I was by no means sure a siege could be withstood.

Iowa State was quite a change from Crown of Thorns. For one thing it was built on a flatland instead of the edge of a cliff. For another, it was elephantine instead of cute. In all directions and beyond counting were formidable gray classroom buildings separated by lawns and quadrangles of ostentatious size. Streams of students who seemed to know what they were doing hurried past Lake LaVerne and the campanile without giving them so much as a glance. This was the big time. My record of straight B's in Bible studies would cut no cheese here. I was awed. What saved me from being overawed was knowing that the Iowa State Cyclones were pitiful in every major sport. How could you be afraid of a school that was the perpetual Big Eight Conference doormat? The teams would have been better dubbed the Doormats than the Cyclones. The school's reputation for academic excellence was based partly on the rottenness of its athletic program. A low value was placed on sports; therefore a high value was placed on scholarship, the thinking went. Whether or not that was true, I don't know. I do know that the University of Iowa at Iowa City sometimes didn't finish last in the Big Ten in football and basketball, which had a lot to do with why students there acted so superior.

Registration was thousands upon thousands of students milling about on the floor of the Iowa State College Fieldhouse in slow confusion, looking for the right lines to wait in and trying to follow printed instructions that ranged from contradictory to opaque. When it was over I found

12

that I had been classified as a New White Male Third-Year Engineering Catholic. The courses I signed up for were Chemistry of Activated Sludge, Solid Waste Management Economics, Sewage Treatment Plant Methods and Equipment, Military Science (ROTC), and a compulsory no-credit seminar given to all engineering students by the philosophy department called Introduction to Civilization Appreciation.

I saw so many girls walking back and forth on the campus sidewalks that I found it hard to keep my mind on my potential career as a top-notch sewage treater and waste disposer. It depressed me to realize that not one of them would be likely to show up in any of my classes. Girls were simply not interested in ROTC or activated sludge. It was going to be awfully hard to meet any of them, and therefore hard to marry them and take them to bed. Taking a girl to bed *without* first marrying her, clerics who had never taken one to bed had assured me for years, was an act of unspeakable depravity that made God fly off the handle more than anything else. Adulterers and fornicators were destined to be punished forever in ways only a being who was omniscient could dream up. God would make life after death so miserable for them they would wish they were dead. The exact nature of the penalty for extra-marital sexual congress was not spelled out anywhere, not even in the Bible, but there was no doubt that it was appalling. Lester Orfenlech, my cousin by marriage from Wahpeton, said that it had something to do with what he called chancres, or putrefied running sores, in the general crotch area. God didn't describe anything so disgusting in the Bible, Lester said, because he didn't want to depress sales of his only book. Lester went on to become an economics major at Fordham.

There were a dozen girls I saw during my first day on campus that I would have been willing to marry without so much as an introduction, that's how magnificent they were. I would have taken a chance on them. The pleasure of being able to come home from school or work every night and fall upon a beautiful woman, to ravish her fully and freely—within the law and possibly with a measure of her cooperation—would easily have outweighed any differences in philosophical outlook that might have emerged later. If a girl is pretty enough, nothing else matters—not stupidity, not communism, not even religious prejudice.

That's what I tended to believe at the time. I had not yet learned that sexual bliss stems less from the quality of the equipment than it does from the manner with which it is manipulated, together with the affection felt for the party the equipment is manipulated against.

The thing that unnerved me most about being a New White Third-Year Engineering Catholic was that everybody I saw was a stranger. I recognized nobody and nobody recognized me. In Dubuque I was always among friends, or at least family. Even at the public high school's football games, where most of the fans were Protestants of one kind or another, there was always a generous sprinkling of people I knew. I wandered around Ames with the notion that I was somehow not the same Tommy Shannon I was before. Previously I had been largely defined by my parents, church, relatives, and peers. What was left, the *essential* Tommy Shannon, was a small part of the total concept. With so much now stripped away I was not fully me, hence not fully responsible for my actions.

The freedom was both thrilling and dangerous. I could have walked around all day with a shirttail protruding from my fly, and what would have happened? Nothing. Nobody would have told my mother. A priest wouldn't have spoken to me in a confessional. I had nobody to answer to, if you didn't count God, and for a few days I was vulnerable. Had I stumbled across a coed studying in long grass, had she looked up and taken an insane interest in my body, she could easily have drawn me down beside her and erased my virginity.

God *did* count, Catholic House was designed to remind me. It was a rambling structure on North Highland Avenue that specialized in boarding Catholic students with nervous mothers. In charge were six Phrygian nuns sent out on a rotating basis from the motherhouse in Windhorst, Kansas. Their habits were floor-length black tents of coarse wool topped off at the sides of their heads by wings of starched linen that flapped when they walked, making them look at times like cans of Dutch Cleanser trying to get airborne. They led us in grace before and after meals and served fish not only on Fridays but on obscure fast

14

days that had meaning only to the citizens of Luxembourg, where in the sixteenth century their order had been founded.

Religious symbols were everywhere: paintings of wan saints looking at the ceiling, stern Christs with eyes that tracked, bloody crucifixes, and crossed fronds from Palm Sunday. On the walls beside doorways were small holy-water fonts into which you could dip a fingertip to make the sign of the cross more potent.

House plants were in profusion. The first floor was like a greenhouse. As Sister Mary Magdalene, our house-mother, explained it, the Phrygians had always had a way with green growing things. Right from the start, the order specialized in truck farming rather than in the more usual teaching, nursing, and contemplation. In Luxembourg to this day they are noted for the size of their carrots and cucumbers. As a way of carrying on their tradition, in Ames they had turned their boardinghouse into an indoor rain forest.

Catholic House was well run, reasonably priced, and conveniently located. In addition, it made me sick. One night during the first quarter, about an hour after I had gone to sleep, I woke up with something wrong with my breathing. There was a faint rattle in my windpipe, like air bubbling through water. I couldn't inhale fully. Clearing my throat by coughing didn't help. Bouncing around and changing my position succeeded only in waking my room-mate.

"Hey, what the hell . . ." he said.

"Excuse me, Lloyd," I said. I was in the lower of double bunks. Any move either of us made was magnified.

I lay still. It was quiet when I held my breath, noisy when I breathed.

"Are you snoring, or what?"

"Must have swallowed something the wrong way. I'll be okay in a minute."

In a minute I was worse. I lifted myself on my elbows and began breathing through my mouth. There was a tight feeling in my chest and upper back. I took in air in short gasps and let it out slowly, making sounds like someone walking through dry weeds. Within five minutes I could hardly breathe at all. Everything inside my chest was constricted. My lungs seemed to have shrunk to the size of teabags. I sat on the edge of my bunk, fighting to get air past the back of my mouth. I felt certain that if I lay down my lungs would choke off completely.

Lloyd groaned, climbed down the ladder, and switched on the table lamp. He studied me to make sure it wasn't a joke, then grew very serious.

"Jesus," he said, "that don't sound good. You might not make it."

He was from a farm near Oelwein and had seen hundreds of barnyard animals die.

"Call . . . Sister . . . Magdalene. She . . . may know . . . a doctor."

"Piss on that," Lloyd said, pulling his pants on over his pajamas. "By the time she gets her headgear on you'll be ready for extreme unction. Get up. We're going to the infirmary."

Was I going to die? Was college going to kill me as it had the Stoody boy in 1932? I started worrying about my mother. Had I been able to speak properly I would have called her and asked her to pray for me. My father claimed that when he was in the hospital with a hernia my mother's prayers generated so much energy that a pitcher of ice water beside his bed exploded. Maybe by aiming more carefully she could clear out my lungs.

The night air was cool and graveyard still. Lloyd wheeled his motorcycle onto the driveway and kicked the engine to sudden life. He revved the engine, setting off a chain of backfires. Lights went on up and down the street. Curses were probably resounding in every bedroom within earshot, but I was indifferent to that. I was near death, perhaps as punishment for religious doubts that lately I had been unable to quash. I clung to Lloyd as we sped toward the campus. I wasn't terrified, though I thought I might have only a few minutes left. If I didn't die of suffocation first, I would be hurled to the pavement and become a grease smear. Darkness would fall in either case. If it stayed dark, if there was no Judgment Day, then I would know that Catholic doctrine was somehow flawed, as I was coming to suspect. If, on the other hand, the darkness lifted and I found myself rising from the dead, my body freed of acne and respiratory ailments, what was to fear in that?

16

Hell, purgatory, and limbo had receded as strong possibilities. Nobody had spoken of them with much conviction since grade school. The worst prospect was unending blackness, the chance that for all eternity there would be Nothing Happening. I couldn't think. I had all I could do to inhale and exhale.

Night-Nurse Barrett at the college infirmary looked sympathetic. I stood wretchedly before her, shoulders hunched and head hanging, trying every few seconds to suck some oxygen into my lungs.

"Hey, this guy don't breathe right," Lloyd said. "Okay if I leave him here and go back to bed?"

"What's wrong?" she asked me.

"I . . . don't know."

She felt my pulse and listened to my wheeze.

"Sounds like asthma," she said. "Do you have asthma?"

I shrugged helplessly and told her I had a touch of it years before, but never anything like this.

"A little adrenaline should fix you up. Put this on and lie down in there." She tossed me a gown and pointed to a room across the hall.

"See you later," Lloyd said as he left. "Gotta get my eight hours."

The sound of the motorcycle was fading in the distance when Miss Barrett lifted my sleeve. Her fingers were cold and professional on my arm. I hardly felt the needle. She checked my forehead with her hand. "Try to relax," she said.

The tightness faded almost immediately. Within two minutes I noticed a decrease in the feeling of congestion and the wheezing. In twenty minutes my chest was clear. I sat up in bed. The lobby was across the hall and I could see Nurse Barrett sitting at her desk.

"I can breathe!" I called to her. "Better now than I could before!"

She came in and gently pushed my head onto the pillow. "Go to sleep," she said. "Tell the doctor about it in the morning." She closed the door behind her.

I fell asleep with a smile on my face, relieved that I had been in no danger after all, judging from Miss Barrett's calmness. Asthma! Maybe some famous smart people had it. I couldn't get over the strangeness of being ministered to by someone other than my mother. I liked it. I liked Miss Barrett. She helped me when I was in need. Visions came into my mind of her as my wife, serving me balanced meals, palpating my stomach, and rubbing my chest with Vicks VapoRub. I wanted her or someone like her sitting at a desk outside my room forever.

The Iowa State College infirmary. It was the only medical building of any kind that I had ever been in that didn't have a crucifix in the waiting room. I got to know it well during my first six months in Ames. I must have set a record for the most admissions and discharges. At least a dozen times I staggered to the desk in the small hours of the morning, gasping and wheezing and pleading with my eyes for a shot of adrenaline. Nurse Barrett became a friend. Eventually she didn't bother with the paperwork of admitting me as a patient; she simply gave me a shot, made me wait until it took effect, then sent me away.

What was I allergic to? The top allergist in Story County tried to find out. He took a detailed history, tested my lung capacity, and made graphs of my breathing. He covered my arms and back with tiny scratches and seeded them with selections from his arsenal of irritants. The results were discouraging. I was allergic to house dust, pollen, feathers, dander, wool, chicken fat, chlorophyll, gunpowder, Pepsodent, rutabagas, milk, wheat, fish, eggs, lanolin, fuchsias, and alfalfa. The implication was that the only way for me to find peace was to move into a sealed bottle with airlocks through which sterilized food could be passed and waste products ejected. The least I could do, the doctor advised, was to make a thorough examination of my present living quarters. Throw out all pillows, blankets, rugs, drapes, pets, clothes, and plants. My room should stress linoleum, plastic, and tubular chrome, and should be located, to be on the safe side, in the kind of dry climate that can be found in northern Chile.

When I saw plants on the list I thought I had the answer. I was wrong. It would have been closer to the truth to say that I was allergic to Catholic House, but even that would not have been precise. I hit upon the culprit after years of studying the etiology of my affliction—when it first struck me, when it was at its worst, when it departed for good. *Etiology* was a word I came across while search-

18

ing vainly for clues in medical books, an approach doomed to failure because most of the available reference works in Ames were aimed at veterinarians. I was not allergic to the woolen habits worn by the Daughters of Phrygia, nor to their Luxembourgian food, nor to the holy water in their fonts. It was more abstract and pervasive than any of those. What I had become allergic to was Christianity itself.

3

Does Prayer Work?

Despite my efforts to suppress them, religious doubts had been undermining the fortress of my faith for years. I was good at arithmetic, and I could see that there were things about Christianity that didn't add up. However, when you lived in a town like Dubuque, where everyone was at least a Christian if not an out-and-out Catholic, you tended not to do anything about it. Digging into weak spots was too risky. A chain of devil's logic could lead you into the cesspool of apostasy, to ostracization, to chancres. There was no way an atheist could have made a living in Dubuque, Iowa, in the 1950's except as a prostitute or thief.

In the entire northeast Iowa area there wasn't a single Moslem, Buddhist, or Hindu. The only man in Dubuque I knew for sure was a Jew was a junk dealer named Hymie Greenbaum, who was regarded as a colorful novelty. There were rumors that Dirty Dan, the ice-cream man who sold cones to children from a horse-drawn cart, was a Jew. I doubted it. He didn't look anything like the other one. While the Chrysler dealer and the Avon lady had suspicious names, I never heard anybody come right out and say they were descended from the killers of Christ.

I once read in an almanac that there were ten thousand Jews in Iowa. Impossible. It made me wonder about the book's other "facts," like coal exports and famous blizzards. The only way so many Jews could have escaped my attention was if they were disguised in bib overalls and baseball caps and distributed evenly across the state's cornfields and pastures, one for every 5.629 square miles (10,000 divided into 56,290), and why should they have gone to the trouble?

The only atheists I ever heard about, aside from Russians and other Communists, were foreign historical figures who had suffered horrible deaths. In grade school the nuns assured us that Russia would be swinging back to God's side at any moment, a miracle to be wrought by a worldwide prayer campaign. Many times I knelt in St. Procopius Church with my classmates, fervently asking the Blessed Virgin Mary to use her powers of intercession with God the Father to bring about the conversion of Russia. The conversion of Russia was a grand, thrilling concept that stirred up visions of masses of people in overcoats and fur hats surging toward communion rails with tears streaming down their weathered faces. If my prayers could have made the dream a reality, it would have given me a wonderful sense of personal accomplishment. It never occurred to me to wonder why the Blessed Virgin needed a bunch of Dubuque schoolkids to call the problem to her attention. Surely the job of being the wife, mother, and daughter of God was not so demanding that she couldn't have thought of it herself.

I also prayed for simpler things than the conversion of Russia. During basketball season I prayed for the conversion of free throws. Reed thin and a fumbling ball handler, my main chance of getting any playing time on grade- and high school teams was to make a good percentage of my foul shots. I was fouled a lot because I was willing to drive for the basket without regard for my safety. Whenever I got the ball I hurled myself into the big guys and hoped that they wouldn't actually kill me. Once on the charity line my practice was to bounce the ball a few times, take a deep breath, study the basket, make the sign of the cross, and whisper, "Jesus, Mary, and Joseph, help me," after which I launched a high, arching bomb. By throwing it high, I reasoned, I was giving the Holy Family plenty of time to guide it through the hoop.

Gradually such thinking began to strike me as foolish. Why should God concern himself with the success or failure of free throws in games between Catholics? He shouldn't be asked to choose between fouled players of equal piety. Where in the Bible does it say that blessing yourself improves shooting accuracy? I wondered if there were any statistics on the accuracy question and whether it would be a sin to gather some. Going beyond free throws to a larger question, was it reasonable to ask God for a Homecoming victory over St. Donatus?

I raised the question during my senior year at St. Procopius High School when we were studying moral dilemmas. After working on my nerve for a while, I raised my hand and kept it raised until Father Grundy recognized me. He was surprised. In religion class I usually kept my mouth shut and my ears open. Father Grundy had hated me since the eight grade. Serving Mass for him I had dropped the altar missal and in my frenzy to pick it up had almost punted it into the apse. Worse, when thinking about it I had snickered during the Benedicamus. He hated other people, too. The very sight of Elbows Hilken seemed to make Father Grundy wish he was an assassin instead of a priest. He once kicked Elbows out of a confessional, humiliating him in front of the penitents who were waiting in line, because he couldn't stand to hear another word. What Elbows was trying to confess was that he had attended the Shriners' circus.

"Notre Dame plays Southern Methodist this Saturday," I said when I had the floor. "Is it proper to pray for Notre Dame to win?"

Everybody laughed, which irked me. I was trying to raise a significant issue.

"You call that a moral dilemma?" Elbows cut in without waiting to be recognized from the chair. Robert's Rules of Order were not part of his weltanschauung. "If SMU wins it will ruin Notre Dame's whole season." He grinned at me like an idiot and rolled his eyeballs upward until only white was showing. For six years I had laughed whenever he did that, but not this time.

"I know that," I shot at him hotly. "I just wondered if it is fair. A football game isn't a life-and-death matter."

"This one is," someone shouted, and everybody laughed again. Father had to call for order. He had a thin, one-note voice that made his lectures and sermons one of the most powerful soporifics known to man.

Father decided to use my question for class discussion, a waste of time as far as I was concerned. I didn't care what my classmates thought. Grundy was the expert; I wanted him to simply give me the answer.

After a lot of talk the consensus of the class was that it was all right to pray for whatever matters to us. We should also pray that what we *think* matters *really* matters and leave it to God to decide whether it does or not. Since God is omniscient, there is no need to worry about taking his attention away from other subjects. Father added in summing up that, in the case of the Notre Dame game, it had to be kept in mind that the great good Notre Dame does as the major Catholic academic institution in the country depended in large part on its financial soundness, which in turn depended on the success of its football team. Therefore, praying for a Notre Dame victory was not only proper, it was strongly recommended.

I didn't pursue it, though I wasn't satisfied, and the problem of prayer continued to haunt me. There was something suspicious about it. When you pray, you are asking God to change his mind—telling God what to do! In early 1949 I and my Crown of Thorn classmates were asked to pray for the Chinese Nationalists. We were asked, in effect, to address God as follows:

Dear God,

The Chinese Revolution is drawing to a close. Unless a miracle happens, the Communists are going to win and the Nationalists are going to lose. Some six hundred million souls are at stake, not to mention mineral rights, hydroelectric power, and cheap handicrafts. A Communist takeover of China, God, would be *very bad news.* Surely you can see that. You don't even have to be omniscient to see that. If you don't watch out, a certain gentleman by the name of Mao Tse-tung is going to be *Numero Uno* in China and the Christian missionaries for the last hundred years are going to see their work go *phfft!* Here's what I want you to do: Intervene directly in the field to turn the tide of battle in favor of Chiang Kai-shek and his wife and her brother and her one good sister. Keep intervening until China is once more safe for the missions. Maybe you have some long-range plan in mind in letting China go down the tubes, but I can't help feeling that recent Communist victories are the result of simple *inattention* on your part. Surely the creation of six hundred million atheists is not part of any *plan*. The time has come, God, for some really sensational miracles.

Yours faithfully . . .

Other things festered in my mind during my two years at Crown of Thorns College, perhaps through the efforts of the Devil. Why was it that the Church had not made more headway in two thousand years? The Creator of the Universe sent his only begotten son to Earth to walk among us. He dictated the Bible, redeemed our sins, established Holy Mother Church, and vested in a well-financed hierarchy the power to bind and loose. To get the Church off to a good start, he provided it with divine guidance that has He dictated the Bible, redeemed our sins, established Holiness the Pope, the power of infallibility in matters of faith and morals when speaking ex cathedra. These things gave the Catholics a terrific advantage over everybody else, yet here we were in the twentieth century up to our ears in Mohammedans, Hindus, Buddhists, Communists, and Jews! If anything, we were losing ground! Something was wrong somewhere. It was one of those things I had begun to think of as a QNYSA—a Question Not Yet Satisfactorily Answered.

Why weren't any big miracles performed anymore? In the old days seas parted, the sun stood still, and people rose from the dead. I wouldn't be nagged by doubt if I could see a few show-stoppers like those.

For some obscure reason the Jews were the Chosen People. Jesus was a Jew; so were Mary and Joseph; so were the Disciples and all their friends. Father Slattery and Father Grundy glossed over the fact that there wasn't an Irishman or a German in the lot. Despite the monopoly the Jews had on the early Church fatherships, the Vatican was in Rome rather than Jerusalem and Mass was said in Latin rather than Hebrew. Why? Because at the time the package was being put together, Rome had the strongest army. Where was the justice in that, theologically? It would have been more direct to make the Italians the Chosen People in the first place.

4

Breakdown at St. Eurythemus

By the time I arrived in Ames to begin my technical studies, I had long since given up blessing myself before free throws. I had cut way back on praying, too. I never prayed anymore in a formal way, on my knees with my hands folded, because while the humbling effect of that posture may have been salubrious, I failed to detect any influence on the results. The results always hovered around the chance level no matter how I arranged my body. I tried a different tack for a while, lying in bed chatting with God informally on a boy-to-God basis. Since he never answered or gave any solid sign that he was even listening, I couldn't help feeling that I was chatting with myself.

Things were different during eighth grade and World War II. During the war everybody prayed like mad and was rewarded with a resounding victory. Later I learned there was more to it. Beating the Axis depended not so much on the superior sanctity of the Allies, but on such secular factors as ammunition, logistics, and mobility. Some military analysts even went so far as to claim that Russia (on whose side it could hardly be argued that God was) had played a significant role. A nation of atheists! Helping to beat two Christian countries like Germany and Italy! If God was going to support anybody, you'd think it would be Italy, where his administrative headquarters had been located for so many centuries. Paul—of Dubuque, not of

Tarsus—before he abandoned the real world and sank into a cloister, came right out and told me that there was more to war than what Mom seemed to think, which was that if you carried enough Bibles, missals, and medals, no bullet could reach a vital organ. Mom also believed that prayer could affect a projectile's trajectory. She did not change her mind when Paul lost a foot with half of St. Procopius parish praying for him, even though Rudolf Hess emerged from the war unscathed.

After the war religiosity ebbed. At some time between 1945 and 1950 everybody came to agree tacitly that it was more important to prepare yourself for a career than for eternity. Religion wasn't abandoned, just put to one side as the important work of cashing in on the postwar boom was attended to. Everybody rushed gleefully ahead except me. For some reason I was bothered by questions none of my friends gave a damn about. Was the Bible the word of God or wasn't it? God may have dictated a long, rambling message to mankind at some point, but how much was lost in translation and typesetting? If a single sentence in the Bible was false, then every sentence could be questioned. Did Christ walk on water and rise from the dead, or were those stories concocted by an overzealous publicist? Were the nuns full of bologna or only partly full? I couldn't relax until I had answers.

During my first quarter at Iowa State, asthma and the serpent of doubt made it impossible for me to concentrate on schoolwork. Current affairs were distracting, too. Senator McCarthy claimed he had uncovered fifty-seven cases of disloyalty in high government circles. United Nations forces in South Korea, under the command of General Douglas MacArthur, smashed out of their Pusan beachhead and carried out an amphibious invasion of Inchon. Al Jolson died in San Francisco while playing cards at the St. Francis Hotel. The United Nations headed toward the Manchurian border, where two hundred thousand Chinese troops waited, grinning. George Bernard Shaw died. On the same day that Puerto Ricans tried to assassinate President Truman by shooting their way into Blair House, the Vatican issued a statement. At last, the chief executive officer of the one, true Church and direct spiritual descendant of St. Peter himself was going to shed some light on the tumult and confusion. But Pius XII, seventy-four, born Eugenio Pacelli, did not share the world's concerns, at least not on November 1, 1950. With Puerto Ricans on the rampage and the Chinese army about to be, the Pope saw fit to proclaim as official Catholic dogma that the body of the Blessed Virgin Mary was reunited with her soul by being physically taken up into heaven. Not a word about Truman's close call, the Korean police action, or Joe Louis's loss to Ezzard Charles. I couldn't believe it—not the proclamation, which I had to believe because it was issued ex cathedra, but the irrelevancy of it, The otherworldliness of it. The press reports didn't include the evidence that drove the Pope to his conclusion. Apparently he came to it during a meeting with the College of Cardinals, the minutes of which were not available to Reuters. I learned one thing from the newspaper accounts, though: The doctrine of papal infallibility dated only to 1870 and was not something Jesus wrote into the original charter.

I sat on a bench for hours staring at unconcerned students hurrying in and out of the student union. Inner turmoil was upsetting my stomach. My personal philosophy—my weltanschauung, if you will—was in a state that could only be called flux.

To avoid slipping into perdition unnoticed, I tried to talk to my roommate. Lloyd wasn't interested. I asked him what his weltanschauung was and he said he didn't have one. I told him you couldn't get out of having a weltanschauung. He said if he had one he didn't want to think about it. He said his girl friend and studying gave him enough to worry about without getting into all that other stuff. My problem was exactly the reverse. All that other stuff was screwing me up completely.

Early in the second quarter, when snow was falling remorselessly, I decided to do what I had promised my mother: visit Father Slattery, pastor at St. Eurythemus in Ames. He knew me and my family from the years he was assigned to St. Procopius. He was a nice man and a happy man. He had a clear mind. He would help me.

Face to face at the rectory door we hardly recognized each other. We had both aged. I was taller and my skin had improved. He was heavier and his hair had turned gray. He took me to his office, a comfortable room with a view of the side of the church. I was greatly honored when he poured two snifters of brandy.

"Should I be drinking this?" I asked, lifting my glass to him. "I'm not quite of age."

He laughed. "We're only breaking a law of man. The laws of God, those are the ones to worry about."

I said yes, I guessed that was right. I said that I supposed he would have to sell it to me before any ordinances were broken. He said that I might have a point there, but said he felt safe, seeing as how we were on church property.

"It sure is good," I said. My lips, tongue, and throat felt as if they had been seared by a poker.

"It's nothing special," he said. "It's good mainly in that it's cheap."

I admitted that I didn't actually know much about whiskey. The conversation sputtered along. After a pause that was a little too long for comfort, Father asked me if something was troubling me or if I was just making a social visit.

"No, no," I assured him, "nothing is troubling me. I don't have any particular troubles. Well, I can't say I don't have *any* troubles. Everybody has troubles of some kind, I would imagine. It wouldn't be natural for a person to say that he didn't have *any* troubles. . . ."

"Suppose you tell me what's bothering you."

I didn't know what to tell him. I didn't know what was bothering me exactly.

"Father," I said after further urging, "I seem to be having some sort of difficulty with my . . . with my . . . well, with my faculties of belief."

"Your faculties of belief?"

"Yes. Things I should believe, that I want to believe, that I used to believe, I'm not sure I do believe."

"Like what?"

"I've always had a few questions in my mind that I figured would get answered sooner or later. My family, the guys at Catholic House, they don't seem to have any trouble believing. I have trouble believing certain things, anyhow. Other things, okay. I'm not talking about other things. I'm talking about the things that I don't doubt I don't ac-

28

cept—I mean, that I can't believe." I was talking too fast, but I couldn't help it. "How do you handle that? I mean doubt."

"Suppose you give me an example."

"It's interfering with my studies, Father. I got terrible grades in the first quarter because I couldn't get my mind off these certain things. Last night I was trying to read a book on the flow of effluent in pipes and before I knew it I was thinking along certain other lines."

"Slow down. What exactly are you talking about?"

"I beg your pardon?"

"Give me one example. One example of something you have trouble believing."

"Let's see. It's hard to say. Sometimes I don't believe one thing, then at other times I don't doubt I don't believe something else entirely." I thought for a minute. "The Immaculate Conception," I said. "And the Virgin Birth."

"The Immaculate Conception and the Virgin Birth."

"And the Trinity."

"The Trinity. You don't believe in the Trinity."

"Sometimes I don't think I do, other times I don't think I don't. There is only one God, but on the other hand there are three Gods. Know what I mean?"

"Yes, I know what you mean."

He rose to his feet and walked slowly to the window and stood there with his arms crossed, gazing into the side of the church.

"The infallibility of the Pope," I said, "And transmogrification."

"Transmogrification?"

"The way the bread and water are supposed to change into the Body and Blood."

"Oh. You mean transubstantiation."

"Transubstantiation, that's it," I said. "There is no chemical test to prove it. It's another one of those faith things."

"You left out indulgences," he said tiredly.

"I did? Well, indulgences. They look a little . . . strange sometimes." I had spilled nearly everything. I felt as if I had vomited on the rug.

Father Slattery, deep in thought, returned to his chair and sat down. He wasn't like he used to be. In the old days he would have slapped me on the back and made fun of

29

what I had said. In the old days he was jovial but learned, too, able to cite chapter and verse to support the helpful advice he gave. There was no merriment now. He seemed infinitely sad.

"I'm scared, Father. I don't know what to do. If my Mom and Dad knew about this . . ." Small salty tears were forming in the corners of my eyes. "Maybe I should start over from scratch. Pretend I'm from Mars and take a course of Catholic instruction as if I didn't know anything. Listen to all the reasons for believing."

"I don't think that's the answer, Tommy. You know the reasons. I gave them to you myself years ago when you were in my religion class." He touched his fingertips and composed his thoughts for a moment with his eyes closed. "The Church is a human institution. We are an association of human beings trying as best we can to do what God wants us to do. Human beings make mistakes. Human beings correct mistakes. Do you pray?"

"Yes. I mean, sort of. Well, no."

"Let me tell you what I pray for. I pray that the Church will change its position on a few things. I pray that God will let the Pope and the College of Cardinals see that times are changing and that the Church must change, too. Indulgences, for example. The official interpretation could be revised one day into something you could more easily accept."

"Really?"

"Certainly. You seem surprised." He sighed. "We've failed you—your teachers have. We've taught you . . . we've taught generations of Catholic students . . . that there is only one truth. That it never changes. That the Church never changes. That it always unerringly reflects God's views. A hundred years ago, when the priest was likely to be the best educated man in town, that image made some sense. Now . . . now people are too smart to be treated like . . . a flock. They aren't lambs anymore."

I stared at him with my mouth open. It was the first time any priest or nun had admitted to me or even implied that the Church was not one hundred percent right in all things at all times.

"The Church has changed before," he continued. "That's why it has survived for two thousand years. I pray for

30

change. I pray that change will come soon enough to keep the Church from becoming like one of its own holy relics. Democracy is what's needed, in my view. The laity should be given a voice. That's the new heresy. I hope the Church yields to it without another war. Otherwise there are going to be a lot of Catholics with terrible choices to make. Catholics caught up in doubt. Catholics like you and me."

"Like *you*?"

"Your problems aren't so unusual, Tommy. When I was in the seminary—that was forty years ago—my roommates and I used to argue about the Virgin Birth and the Immaculate Conception till the sun came up. In a year's time we fought the great heresies of history all over again. We didn't solve anything. When I was ordained I felt that the Church had probably made the best decisions at the time, but that some of them may have been more political than theological. I meant to investigate them further on my own but I've never had the time. When you are a parish priest, counseling, hearing confessions, raising money, believe me, you have plenty of things to keep you busy. You get involved with things that are really bothering people, and let me tell you, it's not the Virgin Birth and transubstantiation. What's the matter?"

I was shaking my head. "It's hard for me to realize that you have any doubts."

He laughed dryly. "Sometimes I even wonder if I should have been a priest. How do you like that? After forty years. I don't think I've done a good job."

"Oh, Father, how could you think that? You've done a *terrific* job. All the kids liked you at St. Procopius. You meant a lot to me, I can tell you that. Not just for the things you said to me in the confessional, but in a lot of ways. My parents liked you, too. They liked your sermons. We always went to the Mass when you were saying it because we liked your sermons better than Father Grundy's. His sort of rambled."

"The things I told you in the confessional I probably got out of a book. Did you know that people sometimes cry right in the confessional? What can I tell them? What can I possibly say that would be equal to the problems they bring me?"

"You can buck up their faith, tell them to ask God for

31

guidance, and sort of give them the long view of eternity and so on so that their day-to-day problems wouldn't seem so important." His eyes were moist. I thought he really wanted my opinion.

"It's an impossible job the priest is asked to do. I'm supposed to counsel people on marriage and family problems and sex, but I'm not allowed to get married. That's one of the Church's biggest mistakes: celibacy. I'm forbidden to get the experience I need to understand the problem."

"This way you can stay objective and not get involved yourself."

"You have to get involved! That's exactly what you have to do! The Protestants are right on this! A priest should have a wife and children just like everybody else!" He slapped the top of his desk in frustration."

"Christ didn't get married. . . ."

"What has Christ got to do with it? I'm not Christ, I'm just Jerry Slattery trying to help people as best I can and not doing a very good job of it. Maybe Christ did get married—how do we know? He disappeared for twenty years."

"I don't know about that, but I do know that you shouldn't worry about whether you are a good priest. For my money you are the best priest in Iowa. You say you don't know how to help people. Why do you think they line up to have you hear their confessions? Because you help them, that's why."

His eyes filled with tears, and when I saw it so did mine. It was the first time an adult had ever been emotional in front of me. I must have been around adults before who were deeply troubled, but none of them had ever let me know about it.

"Tommy, listen to me. Forget the details that are bothering you. They don't matter. They give the Church its flavor, yes, but they aren't the main thing. The main thing is that religion works . . . you can see it in the faces of people at the communion rail. Christ died for our sins, that's what counts, and it's up to each of us to figure out what that means and make the most of it. Don't waste your time on the mysteries, you'll get nowhere. Don't give up on the Church. The Church will change, you'll see. Let us pray. . . ."

To my amazement he fell to his knees. I joined him.

There were tears on both our cheeks. I was amazed because in my experience praying was only done in private or during scheduled rituals. I had never seen anyone fall to his knees and pray *spontaneously*.

"O God," Father Slattery said, his eyes closed and his face uplifted, "hear the prayers of thy children. Forgive me my sins and help me in my unworthiness to act as your servant. This boy came to me in need and instead of answering his call, I cried out to *him*, and he answered me in *my* need. Give me the strength to set myself aside and aid those who come to me. Give me the wisdom to find the right words. Help Tommy Shannon use the fine, questing mind you have given him to fulfill the hopes his parents have for him. They are fine, Catholic people, O Lord, and this is their youngest son. Let your light shine upon him and upon me as well. Help Sister Mary Beatrice in the grave choice she must make. We ask these things in Jesus's name. Our Father, who art in heaven, hallowed be thy name. Thy kingdom come, thy will be done, on earth as it is in heaven. . . ."

I had never been involved in anything like this in my life. We were both sobbing. "Give us this day," I responded, "our daily bread, and forgive us our trespasses as we forgive those who trespass against us. Lead us not into temptation, but deliver us from evil. Amen."

"Lord God almighty, creator of all that was made, forgive us for having offended thy infinite goodness. Wrap us in the cloak of thy power through the Lord Jesus Christ, who reigns with thee in the unity of the Holy Spirit."

The door opened and a cleaning woman poked her head inside. "Oh, excuse me, Father," she said. "Let me know when you're finished and I'll vacuum in here next."

5

Meat on Friday

Dear Mom and Dad,

How's everything in the old home town? I see in the paper you are having some ten-below weather. It hasn't been quite so cryogenic here.

Everything is fine with me. I'm still trying to find out what causes the asthma attacks. The doctor says I shouldn't get them in the winter if I have been following his diet. I told him I haven't eaten any feathers or gunpowder for months! Just kidding—I didn't really say that. He says maybe I'm allergic to cold air! That's a big help, isn't it? Cold air is kind of hard to duck in these environs.

Speaking of these environs, the doc says I should try moving, so I'm looking for a new place. There might be something here in Catholic House that doesn't like me. The doc thinks it might be the fuchsias. I told him how many house plants there were and that the fuchsias are especially ubiquitous.

I know you want me to stay put for religious reasons, but there is nothing to worry about. A person's faith should be strong enough to stand up to a few non-Catholics. If it can't, what's it worth? Look at Saint Paul, Mom. He deliberately went to towns where he was the *only* Catholic! He even went to Rome when it was full of Italians of the most dangerous kind—to wit, heathens and pagans. If he could make it in Rome, I ought to be able to make it in Ames.

Finally got together with Father Slattery. We had a nice talk. I see George Bernard Shaw died.

My laundry is in the mail. Hope you can get it back right away as I am down to my last pair of everything.

Cordially yours,
Tommy

Dear Tommy,

It was a little different for St. Paul. He was a grown man and a Saint when he went to Rome. And the people he was visiting, as I recall, beheaded him. Or was he the one who was crucified upside down? It doesn't matter. Now, Tommy, I know perfectly well that there are many fine people who are non-Catholic but you are far away from home and trying to pursue a course of studies. My main hope is that you are not making a terrible mistake by moving and I am praying to St. Christopher.

The asthma thing—I just don't know. Do you remember Dr. Vincent who your father used to go to for his spine? He said asthma and sinus and that whole family aren't fatal very often. He remembers you as the one with the pimples (though they are nothing like they used to be) and says that you should follow sound medical advice.

Sorry to hear about George Bernard Shaw. I will pray for him. Was he the boy from summer camp whose father was killed by a hay baler?

A man who was in your father's shop yesterday for a haircut while I was there doing the mirrors said that his nephew had asthma and it is not so much a problem of the lungs as it is The Bronchial Tube. It tightens right down, he said. I want you to pray to St. Blase, the patron saint of throat diseases, and I would imagine that includes The Bronchial Tube.

We are glad you went to see Father Slattery. He is a good man with a good brain you can admire.

Your father wants you to do a little study of Ames when you get a chance. He wants to know the number of barber shops for every thousand people and the number of chairs in each one—you know the kind of thing he wants. He says if he ever gets his chain of shops idea off the ground he could include Ames and have an excuse to go and see you when he is hopping from shop to shop—you know how he goes on. Be sure to send him the figures as it will make him happy and he can fuss with them evenings. He is trying to shake the flu.

Did you get the hard-boiled eggs I put in your last laundry? You didn't say anything.

Mom and Dad

P.S. Our poor old dictionary sure gets a workout when your letters come! Don't forget *F*, *G*, and *H* are missing.

Dear Mom and Dad,

I found a swell new place to stay, which is not easy in the middle of the school year. It's in the basement of a bungalow owned by a Mrs. Lurella Parkhurst. If fuchsias were the cause of my asthma I shouldn't have any trouble here because they need heat and light to live! Just kidding, Mom. We are next to the furnace and the place can get actually hot.

I have three roommates and they are great. I did some research and it turns out they are just about the top students in the whole school! There is Wayne Nicholson from Cedar Rapids, Archibald Nugent from Sioux City, and Alex Gold, who has this New York accent that sounds really funny, Mom! He has one of the highest grade-point averages in the senior class! I try to keep my eyes opened and my mouth shut as you and Dad have always taught me and already I've had some long-held obfuscations cleared up.

There is nothing to worry about. I could use a little money, if you don't mind my closing on an eleemosynary note.

With every good wish for your continued success, I am

Tommy

Dear Tommy,

Dad and I were happy to hear that you have found a new place to stay but the basement doesn't sound too good. Keep warm and dry and remember that your health is not all it should be and to let us know if you

36

want us to send the big quilt which would be hard to wrap. When you are feeling strong enough we wish you would try Catholic House again where at least you would have the nuns. This basement idea might turn out to be a mistake. Does water come in?

I'm glad your roommates have good Brains and I'm sure they are good boys and wouldn't do anything wrong but Brains aren't everything although they can help. In the long run good eyesight stands a person in better stead.

Are the Nugent and Nicholson boys Catholic? It would be a good idea to go to Mass every morning because your Faith is your most precious possession in anybody's life.

Your father is working hard but couldn't get to the shop yesterday because of the snow which was probably just as well because he couldn't get to the Legion last night either which must have been a tragedy for that stinking Arnold Gertz. When I see the Gertz's at Mass I can't even look at them he makes me so mad. His nose is getting to look even worse than your father's.

Did you get the eggs?

Your Mom and Dad

In January, at least, the cavelike apartment in Mrs. Parkhurst's basement was dry. Whether it would be during the spring thaw was something else again. To get in you had to lift a trapdoor in the backyard and pick your way down a flight of broken concrete steps. In the darkness at the bottom was a shower nozzle and an Army-surplus toilet. The bedroom was shoehorned behind the furnace and was just big enough to accomodate two double bunks and four small desks. The kitchen was larger. In the kitchen you could actually stretch out if you watched what you were doing. The door of the antique stove was held shut by a hockey stick wedged between the handle and a flap of linoleum on the floor.

While I eventually came to think of my roommates as close friends, we paid little attention to each other at first. They showed me my bunk, told me that the penalty for eating someone else's food was death by freezing, explained the flushing mechanism of the toilet, and that was about it.

37

Archy, Wayne, and Alex no doubt would have preferred someone else to me, but I looked harmless. They had no way of knowing I was a religious fanatic until after they had taken my money. Alex Gold said only three words to me during the first week, and those three words were "Holy shit, Marie." He was looking at the books I had dumped on my bunk the day I moved in, a mixture of sanitary engineering texts and theology, together with a paperback entitled *How to Build an Overwhelming Vocabulary*. The bump on his nose, the kinks in his hair, and the sound of his name told me he was Jewish. That was fine with me. As part of my college education I wanted to meet some Jews and find out what made them tick. I wanted to know what they could possibly have been thinking of when they killed Christ. But Alex Gold and the people he represented would have to wait. At the moment I had a lot of work to do.

The previous afternoon I had presented myself to the college librarian. I had decided to review the basics and put my faith back together from the very beginning. My first-quarter grades had been terrible and I couldn't afford to screw up again, but I had to put first things first. I planned to salvage the second quarter by last-minute cramming.

"Where would I find the books on Catholicism?" I asked. "I mean, the books in favor of it."

She was a woman about the same age as my mother, but with more expensive glasses. She smiled indulgently. "There would be some in History, some in Religion, and some in Biography. Have you checked the card file?"

"It's an assignment. Each person in class was given a religion. I wound up with Catholicism. I have to write a paper on how I would convince a creature from Mars to join it."

"How interesting! I'd like to read some of those papers. Follow me. We'll see what we can come up with."

What we came up with was *Apologia pro Vita Sua* by Cardinal Newman, *A Treasury of Essays on Catholic Themes* by Various Authors, *The Revised Baltimore Catechism* by the Confraternity of Christian Doctrine, and a pamphlet entitled *So You Want to Become a Catholic!* by Judith Fennimore Montalvo. These were the books that

Alex saw when I moved into the apartment, along with those I already owned, like *My Sunday Missal* by the Right Reverend Monsignor Joseph F. Stedman, Director of the Confraternity of the Precious Blood, and *The Holy Bible* by . . . well, who the Bible was by was one of things I wanted to nail down.

Father Slattery said the Church would change as a result of votes taken by the Pope and the College of Cardinals, a deliberative body made up entirely of *human beings*. There was the flaw. Human beings have been known to make mistakes. Perhaps some had been made in the history of Catholicism.

The novel idea that Church doctrine was not fixed made a powerful effect on me: It made me feel as though I had stepped from solid rock into mush. The Church reflected God, so how could it change? Could a being that was omniscient, omnipotent, and omnipresent be omnifickle as well?

It was late February. The doubts raging in my breast had to quelled in time to permit me to cram for second-quarter finals, less than a month away. To speed things up I decided to supplement my library research with two field experiments that would force the fat into the fire. I would skip Mass on Sunday and eat a hamburger on Friday and see if I felt guilty.

The Skipping-Mass-on-Sunday Test

I had never failed to attend Mass on Sunday or on Holy Days of Obligation when I was physically able to go. Absence would have been a sin. Who said so? The Church. There was nothing in the Bible about going to Mass specifically, only a reference to "keeping the Sabbath holy." But the Sabbath, it can be argued, is Saturday! Not only that, maybe the Bible wasn't divinely inspired. Maybe it was a human production entirely, full of irrelevancies, compromises, and blunders, like, say, the Des Moines *Register*.

My plan was to skip Mass under controlled conditions. The last one on Sunday in Ames was at a quarter after eleven in the morning. When eleven arrived on the day of the test, Archy was still in bed. Wayne was at the kitchen table reading the paper. Alex was in our one upholstered chair, working on his toenails. I was at my desk, my goose-neck lamp spotlighting Ernest W. Steel's *Water Supply and Sewerage,* my eyes wandering over paragraph 449, Optimum Conditions for Sludge Digestion, in which it was stressed that incoming raw solids should not exceed 3.5% of the well-digested solids already in the tank. The pH of the sludge, as usual, should be held below 7.4.

I snapped the book shut and switched off the light. "Gotta be going," I said. I put a sweater and coat on and gave my head a few swipes with a hairbrush. On the way out the door I announced that I would see everybody in an hour. "Good-bye," Alex said, not looking up from his feet. "Pray for nookie."

Note that I did not say I was going to Mass. I didn't want to add a lie to the larger sin I may have been committing. I left my missal in plain view on my desk to establish beyond question that my intention in leaving in time for Mass was never for a moment to, in fact, go to Mass. I may have been a scofflaw, but I wasn't a sneak. If my roommates assumed I was going to Mass, they were being erroneous. I had not made an overt identification of my destination, and I had left a plain sign on my desk that my plans were otherwise from what they ordinarily were at that time on Sunday mornings. By this reasoning I was able to do what I was doing without sacrificing any significant portion of my basic decency.

I went to a bench on the shore of Lake LaVerne and sat down. The lake was frozen. The surrounding trees were bare and looked dead. The sky was gray. At eleven ten an impulse came over me to jump up and sprint toward the church. It passed. At eleven fifteen I visualized the priest and altar boys making their entrance from the sacristy into the sanctuary and the congregation rising to its feet. Hardly anybody knew me, so I wouldn't be missed. At eleven twenty I still could have made it . . . I would have been late, bursting in during the Kyrie or the Offertory, but still under the wire. If God wanted to keep my attendance record clean, he would have to give me a sign *now*.

I leaned back on the bench and waited. A girl walked by and glanced at me pleasantly, though not pleasantly enough to imply that I should follow her. I put her out of my mind and thought about myself. I considered my body from head to toe, alert for abnormalities. Pulse, respiration normal. Ears not ringing. No voices, within or without. A cold breeze stung my cheeks, but not painfully. Nature did not grow threateningly silent, nor the air heavy. Neither did any unusual noises arise. No feeling of alarm was sensed in my stomach or any other organ. I listened as hard as I could for some word from God about the rightness or wrongness of what I was doing. I *wanted* a sign. I *wanted* my doubts banished.

God kept Himself hidden. He didn't allow anything to happen that I could have mistaken as a sign. It was quiet there by the lake that morning, but not *strangely* quiet.

At eleven thirty-five I had definitely committed a sin of omission. I crossed my legs, hooked my elbows over the back of the bench, and waited for the feelings of guilt to set in.

My mind wandered. At eleven forty-five I was converting the surface of the lake into an equivalent rectangle, multiplying the length by the width by an average depth in feet and using the conversion factor of 7.48 to get the volume in gallons. What size pumps would be needed to keep that much water circulating to the treatment plant? How much treatment was needed to keep the summer swans from dying? They wouldn't look so pretty floating around upside down, their feet in the air, which is how they would be if the pH of the water was allowed to creep up to 9.4 or 9.5.

Noon came and went. Nothing dramatic was going to happen. It very likely was going to be another lazy day on the prairie. I stood up and stretched, then went back to the apartment.

The experiment was not definitive, but it did tend to suggest that God didn't much give a hoot. Either that or he spoke in a manner too subtle for me to perceive. Maybe I was a spiritual cripple. I felt empty. I wasn't elated for possibly having discovered that I no longer had to go to Mass, nor was I angry that I had gone thousands of times without having to. Emptiness was my only sensation. On the other hand, after a sandwich I didn't feel so empty.

The Eating-a-Hamburger-on-Friday Test

The following Friday, I rode a bus to a diner on the edge of town and ordered a hamburger. I wasn't mealymouthed about it. I looked the waitress right in the eye and ordered a hamburger in an aggressive tone of voice. This was a test and I wanted no mistakes or back talk. I was almost pugnacious. She knew I might be a Catholic who had forgotten it was Friday, but when I spoke out so forthrightly she gave me no trouble. In due course a hamburger was placed before me, along with a few broken potato chips and a carrot stick. I looked around at the other customers. Most of them were eating the Friday specials: Clam chowder and tuna fish casserole. Only one other person I could see had ordered red meat, a woman three stools away who was working her way through a thin steak. She didn't seem to be trying to prove anything by it.

I looked at my hamburger. The meat was protruding slightly from the left side. A drop of grease formed and fell onto a chip. I centered the patty on the lower half of the bun and added a blob of ketchup. With my elbows on the counter I held it in front of my face. It was hard to think of anything as innocuous as a hamburger having any cosmic significance. This particular hamburger was, if anything, more innocuous than most. I rededicated myself to the act I was about to perform. Never in my quasiadult life had I eaten meat on Friday. I was proposing to do so now as a deliberate test of the legitimacy of the ban against it. I opened my mouth and herded the rim of the bun into it. If God was opposed, this was his last chance to let me know. I counted to five, salivating, then bit down.

I chewed alertly. It was delicious! Not ominously delicious and not delicious because it was forbidden. What I was eating appeared to be simply a delicious hamburger in and of itself. Unlike some pleasures, this one carried no hint of a retribution that would follow ineluctably. Nobody turned and stared at me with horror or loathing. I finished the thing in the same anonymity in which I had begun.

I waited a moment before paying the check. I had heard that Jews who had accidentally eaten pork would instantly throw up upon being informed of it. I informed myself that it was Friday and that I had eaten a hamburger. No threatening celestial music came, nor did any nausea. Were the Jews the Chosen People because they had weak stomachs?

On the bus back to the campus I ran through the possibilities.

(a) God couldn't care less.

(b) God cared so much he loaded the meat with trichinosis.

(c) The hamburger contained no meat. I had eaten a clever compound of soy beans, bread crumbs, niacin, and riboflavin. A felonious restaurateur had unintentionally saved me from hell.

(d) I was so depraved I wouldn't recognize God if he grabbed me by the shirt front and shouted, "It's me! It's me!"

(e) I was already dead. Ames was hell.

It was at this stage of my development that my roommates decided to visit a whorehouse. I had no intention of accompanying them at first. The more I thought about it the more intriguing the idea became. Exposure to extreme sexual temptation might be just the thing to bring my program of experiments to a successful conclusion. It would stretch my faith and morals to the breaking point. If there was anything I could do to smoke God out of hiding, visiting a whorehouse was surely it.

I had been exposed to sexual temptation before, of course, but never *extreme* sexual temptation. To avoid offending my own mother as well as the Mother of God, I had so far managed to keep the temple of my body inviolate. At least *other* people hadn't had any fun with it. I had arrived at the Ames bus depot the previous September with more than suitcases, hopes, and an emergency ten-dollar bill; I had my virginity, too. My baggage was spiritual as well as Naugahyde.

6

The Schemers in the Bungalow

If you had been four young men in Iowa in March, how would you have found a whorehouse? We were not stupid, Wayne, Alex, Archy, and I. We were students at a great agricultural college, destined one day to assume leadership roles in animal husbandry, veterinary medicine, agronomy, and sanitary engineering. Having fulfilled the lower division prerequisites, we had been exposed to a wide variety of fact and opinion in the sciences and humanities. What we didn't know, what we had never been taught, was how to find a whorehouse.

Assuming one was found and I tagged along, I made clear to my roommates that I wouldn't *do* anything once we got there. I explained that in my religion sex outside wedlock was a serious sin. I didn't add that in my religion sex *inside* wedlock wasn't such a hot idea either, unless you wanted to be immersed in children. All winter I had presented myself as a quiet, serious Catholic. They knew I was engaged in theological investigations, but they didn't know why. I was afraid I would have been subjected to persiflage or even obloquy had they suspected that the fortress of my faith was suffering from cracked plaster and sagging joists. Alex Gold, the New York Jew, who may have been the most cynical person in Iowa at the time, said that all searches for ultimate truth were bullshit. It was in precisely that kind of search that I was, of course, involved.

"All we want," Alex said one night when the whorehouse expedition was being discussed, "is to satisfy a basic human need for shtupping. Will society make it easy for us? No."

"I was talking to a guy the other day," Wayne said in his usual grave way, "who just got back from Korea. He said you can always get laid over there, even during combat. He scored twice during the Inchon invasion."

"That's Korea," Alex said. "This is Iowa. Koreans have some sense. They're Asians. Asians have a timeless wisdom."

"And some Class A whores," said Archy. Archy was small, with darting eyes set in a ferretlike face. A restless energy drove his words out in short bursts.

We were sitting at the kitchen table. We were almost always sitting, because suspended from the ceiling was a network of fat furnace pipes. Standing was possible only along certain narrow pathways. Dinner was over and the dishes had been carried to the sink and stacked on those from lunch. I was staring at the floor, trying not to show how pissed off I was over what Alex just said about Iowa. He never missed a chance to knock Iowa and religion, no doubt because he knew I was emotionally involved with both. He was obnoxious and he was ugly, and not because he was Jewish, either. He would have been obnoxious and ugly in any religion. Finally I couldn't contain myself. I broke into the conversation and told Alex he wasn't fooling me; I knew the derogatory comparison between Korea and Iowa was for my benefit. I told him I didn't make fun of New York, so he should have the courtesy to lay off Iowa, the subtle beauties of which were far beyond his ken. He was always saying that nobody of consequence had ever come from Iowa, so I set him straight on that once and for all, rattling off the names of Herbert Hoover, Harry Hopkins, Bourke B. Hickenlooper, and James Wilson, a man who served as secretary of agriculture for no less than sixteen years (1897–1913). To the world of sports, Iowa contributed Bob Feller, Jay Berwanger, Welker Cochran, Mickey Marty, and Looper Lynch. In the arts were painter Grant Wood and organist Bobby Gribben. I clinched my case with facts I picked up from a recent Robert Ripley column: Anton Dvorák composed part of his Symphony

No. 9 in D Minor (Opus 95) during the summer of 1893, which he spent in Spillville, a town in northeast Iowa that also has an interesting collection of homemade clocks.

Alex stared at me in astonishment as I made my heated speech, his eyebrows high and his mouth open. When I finished he turned away and covered his face with his hands. His ears turned red. I thought my words had shaken him deeply, then I realized that he was trying not to laugh. He was a geographical as well as a religious bigot. I admired him, though, for not laughing. He regarded me as toweringly ignorant and was trying not to hurt my feelings irreparably. Underneath that repellent exterior was at least a tincture of compassion.

The silence was broken by Archy, and the conversation resumed as if my outburst had been a hallucination nobody wanted to acklowledge. "The library," Archy said, rushing his words. "All human knowledge can be found in the library, if you know how to look it up. They hide the good stuff. So you have to ask the librarian. You look her in the eye and say, 'Where do you keep your fucking directories?' "

"Too vague," Wayne said, who thought he was so smart. The hell of it was, he *was* smart. "She might think *fucking* was an adjective instead of a verb. Better to say, 'Would you direct me, please, to your latest listing of commercial Iowa fuckers?' "

"See what I mean?" Archy said. "You can't ask the librarian."

"All human knowledge is not in libraries," Alex said, scratching his stomach. He strained in an effort to fart loudly, but failed. "What we want is important, part of real life, so the library won't have it." I thought he was planning to ignore me until he added, "Except maybe the Vatican library." He looked at me. "The Vatican has the biggest collection of dirty, rotten, filthy stuff in the world. Isn's that right, Shannon? Could you call the Pope and get a few names and addresses?"

"You keep talking about the Vatican's dirty library," I said. "There is no such thing. Do you believe every lie you hear about Catholics?" There was something about Alex that made me spring to the Church's defense. After fourteen years of Catholic education, I sure as hell would have

46

heard about a collection of dirty books in the Vatican had there been one.

"There are no lies about Catholics."

"What if I said there was a collection of dildos in every synagogue? That would be just as stupid. My word against yours. Catholics believe that pornography is a sin, in case you didn't know. The Pope wouldn't let any within miles of the Vatican."

Alex turned up his palms and looked around the room. "What a shlimazl! I can't believe it!" Then to me: "Would you come home with me next summer? We could make some good money. I know some nightspots in Manhattan that would book you. All you would have to do is stand on the stage and describe your religious beliefs. You'd be a smash!"

Wayne leaned forward on his elbows. He had a sepulchral manner and always spoke very slowly. "These dildos, Alex," he said, "that are stored in the synagogues. They would have to be circumcised, wouldn't they?"

Alex chuckled. "Circumcised dildos! Tiny ones for charm bracelets might go. Lemme make a note of that. . . ."

He had a dream of someday making a million dollars selling things by mail, things like obscenities engraved on pinheads, life-size rubber replicas of celebrities that "Christians" could take to bed, bronzed horse biscuits from the winners of the Kentucky Derby. The day he found out I was Catholic he asked if I could get him a copy of the Church's list of banned books. He was thinking of marketing an anthology called *Favorites from the Index Librorum Prohibitorum*. The Pope's declaration that the body of the Blessed Virgin Mary had risen into heaven gave him the idea for a spring-powered toy church. At the touch of a button a plastic dart shaped like the Virgin would shoot out of the steeple and stick on the ceiling. He planned to call it My Sunday Missile.

A few months earlier I was living in the safety of a boardinghouse run by nuns and going to Mass on Sunday. Now my religiosity was making me a figure of fun, and I was participating, albeit passively, in the planning of a trip to a whorehouse. It was hard to get used to.

Archy unfolded a map and smoothed it flat on the table

47

with sharp, nervous strokes of his hand. Wayne pulled his chair closer and said, "If there is a whorehouse in Iowa, it should by rights be in What Cheer."

"That's just the trouble," Alex said, grabbing the map. "There probably isn't any sex for sale in this whole godforsaken state. Unless you want to diddle a pig or a chicken. Plenty of those around."

Archy brightened. "Let's stop at the first farm and ask if we can rent a pig or a chicken. For crimes against nature."

"I wouldn't put it past you, you little creep," said Alex. He examined the edges of the map. "We've got to get out of state. What have we here—Minnesota? Too many big cold Protestant Swedes. Now you take Missouri. Just the opposite. Everybody there is a hayseed hick who smells of manure. Attar of cowshit. Slobs. No, Missouri is out."

Alex Gold was a bit of a slob himself. He was not only the most profane and blasphemous person I had ever met, but among the homeliest. Wayne Nicholson, on the other hand, was handsome, with a button nose, square jaw, and thin lips. These were the aesthetic standards I had unconsciously learned during my childhood in Dubuque, and I naturally assumed they were universal. My third roommate, Archy Nugent, was, as Alex said, a little creep. Short. Furtive eyes and twitching jaw muscles. A guy you wouldn't trust with your pet chicken.

"There's always Nebraska," Alex said. "Nebraska! Missouri! Iowa! What can you do with places like that? Nothing! I used to go out to LaGuardia just to listen to the names coming over the PA system: Paris! London! Rome!" He slapped his forehead. *"Oy,* what am I doing here? I must be crazy. I could have gone to school in Europe. That's right! I had the chance!" He pretended to sob for a minute, then pulled himself together and applied himself to the map again.

"We are overlooking Illinois," Wayne said. "Illinois is corrupt at every level. If there are sinkholes of misery and degradation anywhere in this great country, they are in Illinois." He looked at the map. "I suggest a river town. Quincy looks about right."

"A river town," Archy repeated, brightening again, "that's a good idea. Drunken sailors off the barges . . .

railroad workers . . . truckers. Bound to be something happening in a place like that. How far is it?"

"About 250 miles. The roads don't look too good. But then, neither does your car. It's at least six hours, plus piss breaks."

Archy leaped to his feet. "Let's go."

Everybody stood up.

"Coming with us, Shannon?"

"I guess so," I said. "For the ride. I'm not going to *do* anything."

Alex shook his head. "If you're not going to do anything, why do you want to come? Wouldn't you rather practice Latin at the Newman Club?"

I didn't tell him I wanted to test my faith. I told him I had never seen a whorehouse and was simply curious.

"You mean you're curious architecturally?"

"No, not architecturally. Come on, let's get the hell out of here."

Alex froze, eyebrows arched. Did he say *hell*? Did the Christ-child say *hell*?

He acted though he had lost control of his limbs, allowing Wayne and Archy to push him through the door.

Yes, the Christ-child had said *hell*. It was the first time I had shown the Antichrist a crack in my foundation.

7

Into the City of Sin

Southward from Ames we plunged in Archy's shuddering jalopy, past Slater and Polk City, through Ankeny without a pause, around the Margo Frankel Woods, pistons pounding, wind in our ears, and vibrations penetrating every secret place. South, south we sped, headlong and heedless, until we were in the very heart of Des Moines itself. We found Highway 163 and turned southeast. Through Pella we went, and on to Oskaloosa.

"We have to turn left if we want to check out What Cheer," said Wayne, studying the map. "On Highway 22 we could also take a look at South English, Kalona, and Lone Tree."

"Gee, those sound swell," said Archy. "Lots of action, I'll bet."

He held the car to its southeast bearing, which took us past William Penn College, through Ottumwa, and into Fairfield, home of Parsons College. We just missed Rome, but we saw most of Mount Pleasant, home of Iowa Wesleyan. Quiet towns with streets shaded by elms, maples, and grain elevators. We were in the corner of the state now, just a hundred miles from Quincy, Illinois, fabled river city of exotic delights.

The passing snow-splotched farmlands were flat and outlined by rows of budding trees. Cattle watched us pass through barbed-wire fences. As we neared the Mississippi

50

the countryside became more rolling and wooded. Grasslands, hedgerows, fields of dark earth, and a distant steeple or two presented several splendid vistas. If I had been ten years older and not a virgin en route to a whorehouse, I would have appreciated the scenery more.

We roared through wide spots called Argyle and New Boston without slowing down, leaving in our wake knots of startled farm hands on street corners and swirling funnels of dust. Across the Mississippi we went on the great Keokuk Erector Set toll bridge. We were in totally corrupt Illinois now, heading straight south on Highway 96 at a steady sixty miles an hour . . . through Lima without looking either way, through Marcelline without knowing we were there. Archy kept his eyes on the road. There were beads of sweat on his forehead and a song in his heart. He waved off our offers to help with driving, explaining that to keep his throbbing machine on line took an iron will that only he possessed. That was almost true in Iowa, where the narrow two-lane highways featured sloped curbs on both sides, curbs that, apparently, were designed to help cars go out of control if they strayed too close to the shoulder. If you tried to swerve off the road to avoid an oncoming truck, the curb forced you back onto the pavement to take your punishment.

"Won't be long now," said Wayne. "Five minutes at the most."

"How do we find what we want when we get there?" Archy asked. "There won't be any signs. Look how dark it is already."

"Jesus Christ," said Alex, "you just ask somebody. Anybody. If there's a red-light district everybody will know where it is—men, women, and children."

"Ask a complete stranger on the sidewalk?"

"Why not? Say, 'Excuse me, sir or madame, I seem to have a hard-on. Would you mind pointing me toward the nearest whorehouse?' Or maybe 'My friend Shannon here has a hard-on.' "

"Leave me out of it," I said. "I'm just an observer."

"I'll drive around town first," Archy said. "I have a nose for this sort of thing."

Alex turned to me. "Let me get this straight," he said. "You are not going to do anything when we find the girls?"

51

"That's right."

"Why not? You don't like girls? You are queer? You are short of money? I could loan you ten bucks."

"You know why not," I said. "Because Catholics believe that fornication is a sin." I didn't want to say *flatly* that fornication was a sin because I didn't want to appear to be an extremist. I didn't say that *I* believed it was a sin because I wasn't sure exactly what I believed. The statement I made, that Catholics believed it was a sin, was indisputable and presented Alex with no weaknesses to attack.

"Tell me something," he said, undeterred. "If God is against sex, how come we were born with these big hangin' shlongs?"

"Sexual intercourse is for procreating the race," I said.

"And for having fun," Archy said, peering through the windshield at the dim streets of Quincy. "Doesn't it say anywhere in the Bible that screwing feels good?"

"Explain the sin part," Alex said. "That's what I don't get."

"You just want to make fun of whatever I say."

"I swear I don't. I want to hear it explained, that's all. I never met anybody who believed it before."

I told him that God, through the teachings of Jesus Christ and the inspired writings in the Bible as interpreted by the Roman Catholic Church, had made it plain to mankind that sex was to be confined to marriage. Anybody who broke a law of God committed a sin. If you died with the black mark of sin on your soul, you were punished in the flames of purgatory for a length of time proportional to the gravity of the offense. For what was called a "mortal" sin, as opposed to the less serious "venial" sin, the punishment was hell, from which there was no possibility of parole.

"Why can't you fuck up a storm tonight and confess it tomorrow? You could find a priest right here in Quincy who would wipe the slate clean for a five-spot."

"You don't pay priests to hear your confession, and you don't pay for absolution. Absolution comes if you confess your sins fully and are sincerely sorry for them and if you make a good act of contrition. You can't be sorry if you were planning in advance to use the sacrament of confession as a way out. You would be committing another sin by lying to the priest."

"So you would get another ten days in the flames tacked on to the end of eternity?"

"I told you you just wanted to make fun of me."

"Wait a minute. You say God will lower the boom on you if you take your peter out of your pants and do something with it other than take a piss. Is that right?"

"Outside of marriage."

"Outside of marriage. Now, who told you that? God? Did God tell you that Himself?"

"Well, the Church."

"You mean a bunch of old Italians. Who told them what God wants you to do with your peter? St. Peter? Did St. Peter tell them what to do with their peters? Is that why he is called St. Peter?" He laughed; I didn't.

"If you trace it back," I said, "God told them, and the Church is more than a bunch of old Italians. There's the College of Cardinals, the laity, the hierarchy, the Communion of Saints . . ."

"Who *told* you that God told the old Italians what you could do with your peter? Did God tell you Himself or was it the old Italians?"

"God has never talked to me Himself about anything specific, but I've felt his presence. When you receive the Holy Eucharist at Communion his presence is very strong."

"Lay off, Alex," Wayne put in, "the kid is entitled to his religion."

"But I've got him by the balls now. If it is the Italians who tell Catholics that God doesn't want them to have any fun with their peters, then it's just their word against mine. If the Pope and all those old geezers he appoints say that God tells them what to do, they might be lying or hearing things. Shannon is accepting hearsay evidence. If he is missing out on all the fun because of evidence that wouldn't be admitted in a court of law, he's crazy. And if he says that God is talking to him personally about his shlong, then he really *is* crazy."

I refused to continue the discussion. I didn't want to give him the satisfaction of admitting that there was anything valid in his arguments, and I didn't like the image I was presenting of myself as a Sunday-school teacher. I shouldn't have been drawn into it at all, but Alex was such a Lucifer that even an agnostic would have wanted to brandish a crucifix.

"Great baskets of catshit," said Archy, "what kind of town is this? It's Saturday night, for chrissakes. Where is everybody?"

We had been cruising around up and down the gloomy streets for half an hour, looking for signs of life. Even what was meant to be the main drag was almost totally deserted. At the end of each block a tiny streetlight brought into ghostly view the outlines of low, sullen buildings. The river must have been near because the air was heavy and damp and smelled of aging fish. Archy rolled to a stop outside a nearly deserted neighborhood bar. Inside we could see a fat woman sitting motionlessly on a stool, her back to a man who was slumped over a table, his head on his arms. An extremely old bartender was peeling what appeared to be an apple. They turned and looked at us with expressions of dull-witted puzzlement.

"Sin city," Wayne said.

"So this is Quincy," said Archy, "brawling, wide-open river town. Holy Christ, give me Des Moines to this."

"Maybe the whole place is some kind of historical monument," Wayne said, "carefully preserved to show what things were like before there was life on earth. The *real* Quincy might be farther down the line."

"Lemme out," said Alex.

"Where are you going?"

"I'm going to ask those nice people in the bar where the grab-ass is played around here."

I followed him to the door to make sure I didn't miss anything.

"Excuse me," Alex said with a friendly wave, "I wonder if you could tell me where we could find a little action."

The fat woman swiveled around on her stool. The bartender lowered his apple.

"My colleagues and I have come a long way," Alex said, "all the way from Ames, Iowa, hoping to find some fun. We figured that this being a river town there would be quite a bit of nightlife and so on."

54

"That's some accent," the woman said. "Where you from, France or someplace?"

"New York. Bronx."

The bartender moved closer, keeping one hand on the bar for support. "What did he say he wanted?"

"He wants action, Stanley. He and his friends drove all the way from Ames, Iowa, looking for action. To Quincy. To Quincy looking for action." She smiled.

"Ames?" said the bartender. "Ames? Never heard of it. It's not around here, I know that."

"Stanley," the woman said, "finish your apple before it gets rusty."

"Look, lady," Alex said, "I don't mean any offense, but what we are looking for are some girls. Professional girls."

"Professional girls?"

"Yes. *Filles de joie,* as we say in France. Prostitutes. A house with a red light out front."

She laughed heartily, a jolly pile of flesh in a flower print dress. "Well, for Pete's sake," she said, "if this don't take the cake." She turned to the bartender and gestured to Alex, to me in the doorway, and to the car outside. "Stanley, these boys here are looking for a whorehouse."

"That's it, you got it," Alex said.

"They drove all the way from Ames, Iowa, looking for a *whorehouse.* All the way to *Quincy!*"

Stanley smiled a gummy smile. "A *whorehouse?* Here?" He began cackling. "Son, you took the wrong highway entirely."

"Yeah, well, there was a mistake all right. Somebody told us Quincy. They must have meant Muncie. Or Cincy."

"He walks in looking for action," the woman said, wiping her eyes with the back of her hand. "Isn't that the limit? The best show in town tonight is right here, wouldn't you say?"

The old man was chuckling amiably, his eyes glistening. "Afraid I didn't catch that one, Linda," he said.

"This may be fun for you," said Alex, "but I have a serious problem and I need help. There are some dangerous people with me—caged animals." He noticed me at the doorway. "Like Shannon, there. He's so desperate for a woman I don't know what he might do. Attack a fireplug or something. Look at the spittle in the corners of his mouth."

"That right, sonny?" she called. "Looking for a woman?"

I shrugged.

"Can you help us out?" Alex asked Linda. "Steer us in the right direction?"

She applied herself to the problem. "Stanley, where would these boys find a whorehouse? Springfield?"

"A whorehouse? You'd have to go up the state capital for that. That would be Springfield. Nothin' closer I ever heard of." He pointed at the man collapsed at the table. "Gene there would know. Too bad you didn't come in a couple of days ago, before he started in."

"Springfield, eh? How far is it?"

"Depends on what you're driving," said the old man.

"About a hundred and twenty miles," said the woman.

"Thanks a million," said Alex. "Give me a call if you're ever in Ames."

We piled into the car.

"Where to?" asked Archy.

"Springfield," said Alex, "and step on it."

8

How to Fight Sex

And so it came to pass that four students from Iowa State College—three blaspheming atheists of mixed backgrounds and one Catholic whose faith was perforated but holding—sat down in the pleasant parlor of a whorehouse in Springfield, Illinois.

The Catholic was, to be frank, terrified. All his life he had been given to believe that sex was dirty, evil, foul, and filthy, an insult to mothers and sisters everywhere, a slap in the face for the infant Jesus, and a kick in the balls for God the Father. Adultery! Fornication! The very words were enough to make you sick. Any man who would take the holy vessel of a woman's body, the vessel in which Jesus Christ Himself gestated, and violate it like a common beast of the barnyard, not to procreate the race but merely to satisfy his lust—well, it was only right that such a man be visited by the most horrible diseases imaginable . . . chancres, ruptured testicles, lingering death, and eternity spent in the hottest flames of hell. These were the images raised in my mind years before by Father Breen, a retreat master who apparently was sent from Ireland every two years to terrorize the Catholic schoolchildren of Dubuque.

Retreats normally lasted two days and involved shuttling back and forth between the high school, where we meditated and prayed with the help of approved pamphlets, and the church next door, where we heard sermons on such subjects as the Holy Mysteries; the Meaning of Mary; Materialism versus Reality; the Vocations; and Love, Youth, and Marriage. It was the last topic, love and marriage, that scared us half to death. It was taken up in the gymnasium rather than the church because of the distasteful nature of the subject matter, and the boys were segregated from the girls. Maximum security precautions were imposed. When the girls were in the gym the boys were kept busy singing hymns in the church, and boys sneaking away in hopes of eavesdropping at the gym found priests standing guard at every door.

Father Breen was a spellbinding speaker. He was tall and ruddy-faced, with black curly hair and bushy eyebrows. When, as a freshman at St. Procopius High School, I took my place for the first time with the boys for what was called "the final hour," I was as tingling with anticipation as anyone. Nobody who had made a retreat before would volunteer any details. They had been sworn to secrecy under pain of mortal sin. Smirks, nervous laughs, and knowing looks were the only clues I had.

One reason for the lack of advance information is that it was hard to remember exactly what he said. Father Breen's words were so stunning that our minds tended to block them out. The emotional effect remained, but not the words themselves. It took my friends and me hours of effort to reconstruct his statements.

The opening hit me like a branding iron. We were sitting expectantly in our folding chairs, watching his every move. He was at the side of a raised platform, fussing with some papers on a table. The nuns who had guided us to our seats had left and the doors had been locked. His eyebrows began quivering, and as we tensed ourselves he whirled and faced us, his eyes those of a madman.

"Each of you," he shouted, riveting us to our seats with an accusatory finger, "has between his legs an instrument of terrible power! An instrument that can populate the world and fill the heavens with souls to worship God, or that can drag you down into the slime of despair and the black pit of deadly sin." I was fourteen years old. I had had only six dates. "Your organ of sex can provide you with a Catholic family to the glory of God, or . . ." and here he paused with devastating effect, finishing his thought with a whisper ". . . or it can *destroy* you, destroy your *life* as well as your immortal *soul*."

This was shocking stuff. Never before had I heard a member of a religious order use phrases like "between your legs" or "organ of sex." The nuns and priests who were our teachers had cautioned us about the dangers and evils of the flesh, of course, but always without reference to any particular erogenous zone. They were too embarrassed to deal with specifics, and the same was true of our parents. Father Breen wasn't embarrassed; he was mad. His direct attack, his blitz, left me shattered for months. He knew so much about me! He knew how the terrible instrument between my legs was plaguing me by standing up at odd hours of the day and night, demanding attention; he knew about the guilt-soaked pleasure of masturbation and about the changing character of my dreams. God must have been talking to him about me! As he strode back and forth, gesturing, posing, and glaring, I half expected him to mention the disgraceful way I fantasized about Gretchen Schwartz shinnying up my drainpipe.

We are trapped during our stay on earth, he said, in a body whose design was fouled up by the Devil. It was the Devil who, during a moment's inattention by God during the labor of creating Adam, managed to attach an illusion of pleasure to the reproductive act in hopes of diverting men away from their task of attaining heaven. God noticed what had happened in time to save women from the same fate, but boys and men were left to battle all their lives against base physical desire. This could be turned to advantage, luckily, by using it as an opportunity to show God how much you loved him. By self-control and self-denial men could earn a high place in heaven.

Venereal disease, he explained, is an expression of the Devil's impatience. Unable to wait to impale fornicators and adulterers on his ghastly spits, he covers them with sores and stench while still they walk the earth. This is permitted by God because it is simple justice and because it serves as a deterrent for the yet unsullied.

The function of the female fornicator is to pass along venereal disease to as many males as possible. A girl who opens the gates of hell for a slavering boy so that he can indulge himself in a moment's illusory pleasure is, we can be sure, providing the same service for every boy weak enough to take the first step. We shouldn't be led to think we were "special." It is not in the nature of female fornicators to be selective, whatever they may say. The male fornicator, too, once having violated the sacred vessel of a woman's body, tends to want to violate every sacred vessel he can get his hands on. Not taking the first step, then, was the key to chastity.

Few freshmen and sophomores at St. Procopius High School knew any female fornicators. Most of the girls couldn't even go out at night. To the best of my knowledge everybody in my class was a virgin, with the possible exception of Wanda Farney, who came from a poor family and whose father had once been in jail. But if any of us had accidentally encountered a despoiled person our defenses would have been well-nigh impregnable, thanks to Father Breen. He armed us with weapons designed to enable us to emerge victorious over dangerous situations, evil thoughts, and erections. I can remember his advice because he went over it twice and because I heard him make the the same presentation almost word for word two years later.

By a dangerous situation he meant one in which you were alone with a girl for a long enough time to permit flaws in your character to emerge. Situations were especially dangerous after sundown, if a flat surface was available, and if lewd touches had occurred in the past. Because the Devil's power is enormous under such conditions, the best tactic is to avoid them entirely. If you feel any physical attraction at all for your girl friend, never allow yourself to be alone with her, certainly not at night. Date her for group activities only, preferably those with adults present. If you find it hard to dispel unchaste thoughts about her, she must be dropped entirely until you have brought yourself under control. A good general rule: Don't date any girl more than twice. Father gave us a slogan to memorize: "Familiarity breeds attempt."

Engaged couples were treading the edge of a treacherous precipice. Young people planning a honeymoon, when sexual congress would be more or less forced upon them by custom whether they relished the prospect or not, sometimes drifted into regrettable intimacies because of an unhealthy preoccupation with the physical side of their pending matrimonial relationship. Perhaps through a desire to put behind them an obligatory rite they fear may be degrading and even painful, they quite understandably "want to get it over with." They yield to temptation *before* the nuptials, thus losing their souls through a simple error in timing.

Evil thoughts are best combated by reacting instantly to drive them out. Don't indulge them for a second. If a dirty thought invades your mind, kick it in the gutter where it belongs. If it keeps crawling back, make a conscious effort to lose yourself in thoughts of a favorite activity—golf, basketball, or hockey. It may become necessary to actually putt, dribble, or skate. Try thinking of your dog or your mother. Keep busy is a good rule of thumb. "An idle mind is the Devil's workshop" is as true today as it was when Moses coined it.

Erections are a pesky problem. Fortunately most erections stem from dirty thoughts. Quash the thoughts and you've quashed the erection. Erections are especially vulnerable to vigorous calisthenics. Push-ups, of course, are out, but deep knee-bends, toe-touching, and jogging in place are effective and can be resorted to even in crowded buses without arousing undue suspicion. Young people are expected to be restless and energetic.

Except by a doctor in cases of pathology, an erection should never be touched. That way lies disaster. That way lies the insidious evil of self-pollution. Leaving aside the sin you commit by masturbating, there is the physical harm you do yourself. It saps your strength and makes you unfit for sports. It destroys the zest for life that is the birthright of every human being. It causes the skin to take on a sickly pallor. It puts an intolerable strain on the vital tissues of the lower abdominal region. The violence involved in auto-manipulation injures many delicate membranes and ducts—in fact, it rips some of them from one end to the other. Urinating becomes painful and blood appears in the stool. Finally, and in some respects worst of all, the boy who wastes his seed may one day find himself without any when the obligation has been placed upon him to raise a Christian family and fulfill a woman's destiny.

It boils down to this: An erection symbolizes a contest

between you and the Devil. Interested spectators are your parents, your guardian angel, the nuns, and God. You can play along with the wishes of the Devil and let him draw your hand down, down, down to do his dirty work, or you can by an effort of the will force the Devil and your organ to kneel in defeat. The choice is yours: Eternity in hell or eternity in heaven.

At age twenty, relaxing with my friends in the parlor of a whorehouse, I was a much different person from the lad who stared wide-eyed at Father Breen. I had learned through personal experience that not everything he said was strictly true. Years of almost daily glimpses, for example, had never revealed blood in my stool. While my own virginity was still intact, at least half of my friends in the last year or two had gained carnal knowledge without suffering from nervous breakdowns, chancres, or leprosy. Far from losing their zest for life, they seemed, if anything, more ebullient than ever.

What compromised Father Breen's credibility most was the mistake he made when returning two years later to give another retreat. Through some sort of clerical error, he delivered the same "final hour" lecture to us again, complete with the identical finger pointing, whispering, bellowing, and eye flashing. The discovery that what I had taken to be spontaneous passion was only acting affected me deeply. From then on I felt twinges of doubt almost every day.

Now I was deliberately subjecting the monolith of my faith to the hazards of a house of prostitution. Would it gain strength by resisting the storm, or would it crumble to rubble?

For years and years I had fantasized about what sex was like. Always I had avoided taking the first step for fear of sinking into depravity and parenthood. Now I would meet people who did it over and over! For a living! As a job!

9

An Obscene Gesture

The brothel was ordinary, a two-story wooden-frame house on a nondescript street. On one side was a small parking lot and a grocery store, on the other a row of low-rent rooming houses. The parlor was not much different from the one at Catholic House. We sat on overstuffed chairs and sofas that were mismatched but not shabby. The only clue to the nature of the premises was an enormous oil painting of three portly nude females frolicking on a lawn and pelting each other with pussy-willow switches under the gaze of a stallion with flaring nostrils.

I didn't get it.

Incense was burning somewhere. A car went by outside. A clock ticked. The sound of women's voices and high heels could be heard approaching. Archy was breathing deeply, his hand pressed on his crotch as if trying to suppress an eruption. Alex looked at me and grinned. Moisture appeared on my nape.

Three women came into the room. "Hi," they said. They seemed friendly. I thought they might be hostile, blaming us somehow for contributing to their debasement. I rose, then sank down again, wondering if by standing for prostitutes I had committed a terrible gaffe.

They were younger than I thought they would be, and better looking. Their hair looked hastily pinned up and their faces showed signs of sleep. All three wore silk robes loosely tied at the front. Thank God they sat next to the other three guys. I stared at them unabashedly, almost unable to believe that they were there, or that I was there.

"Jeez," said the one sitting on the arm of Archy's chair, "can't you guys wait until a decent hour? When's a girl supposed to sack out?"

"Sorry," said Alex. "We went to eleven o'clock Mass and the sermon ran on a little longer than we expected."

Somebody chuckled briefly.

"Funny," said Wayne, "you don't look Catholic."

"Yeah, and besides," said Archy's girl, "there is no eleven o'clock Mass. If you miss the one at ten you have to wait till twelve." She looked down at Archy, at the strained expression on his face, at the hand pressed to his crotch. She lifted his hand and replaced it with her own.

Archy jumped to his feet.

"Follow me," she said.

They left.

The woman next to Alex raised her arms and yawned. Her robe fell open, exposing her legs to the hips. From where I was it didn't appear that she was wearing anything underneath. Alex touched her thigh. She whipped her gown shut. "No free samples," she said.

Alex whispered something to her with an evil smile. She whispered something back. He whispered. She whispered. I would have given anything to know what they were saying. Finally Alex stood up and said, "It's a deal." They strolled out hand in hand like Jack and Jill.

The third prostitute sat on the sofa next to Wayne, looking at him with interest, her legs crossed and her chin in her hand. "I think you are the handsomest stud that ever came in here," she said. "I'm almost glad Sheila woke me up."

Wayne laughed. "What will that cost me?"

"That's free."

"What else is free?"

"There's a dish of peanuts on the mantel. Come on, I want to show you some things in my room."

"You mean you won't do it for love?" Wayne winked at me.

She smiled becomingly. She didn't seem at all depraved or wretched. She had a good personality.

Wayne let her take his hand and pull him to his feet. She led him through the door. "Oh, why not," he said. "I've come 250 miles already . . . might as well go the rest of the way." Despite his effort to project sangfroid, I'm positive he was blushing.

The instant I was alone a feeling of panic came over me and my heart started beating wildly. I looked back and forth, trying to remember where the front door was, wondering if I should bolt outside and sprint in any direction till I dropped from exhaustion. If the door was locked I could dive through a windowpane and hide in the car until the sinning had stopped. What would Christ do? He wouldn't make a run for it or hide in a car. He wouldn't relax in an easy chair, either, not while three of his disciples were consorting with common harlots, diddling themselves into oblivion and more than likely dosing themselves with clap to boot. No! He would stride with indignation to the cubicles and cribs, denouncing the couplers as he had denounced the Gadarine swine.

"Are you the only one left?"

A young girl had come into the room holding a cup and a saucer. She couldn't have been more than nineteen years old, and her pigtails and schoolgirl dress made her look even younger. She was by no means pretty. Her legs were too thin, her hair was stringy, and her cheeks carried the faint remains of acne. She reminded me a little of a onetime sweetheart, Ellen Ettelsly, but her hair wasn't as shiny and her teeth needed work. I thought she was the madam's daughter or maybe a niece who came in to help with the dusting . . . until I noticed the way she was dressed. Her dress was too short for anybody's niece or daughter, and it had a zipper running from top to bottom down the front. This wistful thing was a goddam whore!

"Wait till I have a cup of coffee," she said. "Can I get you one from the kitchen? I made it myself."

"No, thanks, I don't drink coffee." The sound of my voice startled me, it was so high and small.

"How about a cigarette?"

"I'm afraid I don't smoke, either," I said strongly, forcing my voice into a lower register.

"I can't start the day without coffee and a cigarette," she said. She lit up deftly and flicked the match toward the fireplace. Taking a deep drag, she walked cup in hand to a window and pulled back one side of the venetian blinds. "How's the weather? Hope it stays nice until tomorrow. Going for a boat ride. Where's your car? Did you walk?"

"The last couple of blocks. We drove all the way from Ames. The car broke down."

"Ames, Iowa? You guys from Iowa State? I went to Colorado for a while. Didn't like it. Well, I liked some of it."

She sat down and busied herself with her coffee and cigarette. She hardly glanced at me since coming into the room. I tried to think of something sociable to say.

"What was your major?" I finally came up with.

"Darned if I remember. My father signed me up for something. I didn't go to class much. The last two weeks I lived like a queen in the attic of a fraternity house. I made over a thousand dollars. You've heard of the Sweetheart of Sigma Chi? You're looking at her."

She drained her cup, stubbed her cigarette, and turned her attention to me. Dread grew in my stomach like a tumor. My hands tightened on the arms of my chair. Looking into her pale blue eyes, it was hard to believe she was a female fornicator. She looked like somebody's sleepy young sister.

"What are you majoring in?" she asked.

I was tense as a spring. She was trying to put me at my ease, and my heart went out to her for that. She was just a kid my own age! How had she gotten herself into this cesspool? How many mad dogs had ravished her thin body, which she should have been holding inviolate for the sacrament of matrimony? I wanted to grab her shoulders and shake some sense into her, try to make her realize the terrible sinfulness of what she was doing. You're too young for this rotten business, I wanted to shout. You could straighten yourself out! You don't have to be a cheap slut all your life! Yet, at the same time, I wanted to kiss her eyes and nose and mouth. If I didn't, somebody else would. I wanted to do these things even though there was absolutely nothing sexy about her except the implied promise that the secrets of her body could be mine in exchange for a piece of green paper. A vision of the two of us writhing on the floor dissolved into my mother sobbing. I felt shame. This girl almost certainly didn't love me. She was

66

the female fornicator I had been warned against, and here I was, thinking of gaining fleshly knowledge of her. What kind of man-boy-beast was I? I vowed not to succumb! I reached inside myself and found deep pools of moral strength, pools fed by a lifetime of Catholic education. I would not debase myself or my manhood or her or her womanhood or our larger shared humanhood by taking part in a sordid sexual spectacle. I tried to think of base-ball, basketball, hockey, eight ball, my dog, and my mother.

"I asked you what you were majoring in," she said. "Relax, for gosh sakes, I'm not going to bite you."

I lowered my hands and looked at her. She had some very nice qualities.

"I'm majoring in sanitary engineering," I said.

"And just what would that be?"

"Sanitary engineering? Well, it has to do with waste disposal, sewage treatment, designing sewerage systems, and that sort of thing. Sewage and sewerage aren't the same thing, you know, which is kind of an interesting point right there. 'Sewerage' is the network of pipes and 'sewage' is what is carried *in* the pipes. See? Every town has a whole system of buried pipes to take sewage away from homes and factories to a sewage treatment plant. Most people don't even think about it, but there is a lot of engineering involved. It's not dull by a long shot, if that's what you're wondering. It can be awfully darned interesting. Did you know that garbage and waste are growing faster than the population? It's true. We would soon be buried in the stuff if engineers didn't keep ahead of it." I was talking too fast and running my words together the way I always did when I was scared out of my wits. "Treating the sewage once you get it to the plant is a whole other thing in itself. We are working on ways to purify sewage so that it can be re-turned—actually pumped back into the intake of the water supply system, which would take another network of pipes that somebody has to design—and used again. I mean we would actually drink it and it would be perfectly all right."

"Is that so? Let's go to my room and take off our clothes."

"Ma'am?"

"You need some loving and you need it in a hurry." She

took a few steps toward the door, beckoning to me with a toss of her head. "Come on, let's do a little hugging and kissing and see what happens."

Words I thought I would never hear. Part of me wanted to race to her room and buy everything she had to offer, and part of me hung back. By hesitating I was saved. In the great road of life I had arrived a treacherous fork and I chose the tine of righteousness.

"No," I said, a man of steel. "This is a fork in the road, and farther along I don't want to have to look back and see that what I was saying I didn't believe myself—I mean about being along for the ride and my whole self concept having to do with my moral fiber and the courage of my convictions. Those are the things that count in the long run. I'm talking about myself now and you and me, not sanitary engineering."

"You don't wanna? You come all this way and now you don't wanna?"

"I didn't say I didn't wanna. What I said was that I'm not gonna."

She folded her arms and shook her head. "You don't drink coffee and you don't smoke and you don't screw. You should at least chew some gum some day, just to see what it's like. Would you rather have somebody with big tits? I'll wake up Heidi if you want."

"No, no, no. This has nothing to do with endowments. I think you are very attractive and I'm sure I would enjoy . . . going all the way with you. It's a personal matter in that I think that if a person expects his wife to be a virgin, then it's not fair for him not to be one, not to mention the religious thing, which I could never live down."

"Yeah, well, if you're ever in town again and you want to do it instead of just shoot the breeze, let me know. The name's Dizzy Denise."

She turned to leave, meeting Alex and Wayne at the door. She told Alex that I had "chickened out" and that it was a waste of time. She was going back to bed and catch up on her sleep, she said. Alex began whispering to her. Wayne sat down, put his head back, and closed his eyes. I heard Denise say it was no use. Alex persisted, apparently trying to persuade her to do something. They glanced in my direction once or twice. Before I had a chance to congratulate myself on the strength of my moral fiber, my apprehension and sense of impending doom began to grow again. I think Alex gave her some money, but he had his back to me and I couldn't be sure. What I know for sure is that Denise shrugged and walked toward me. I rose to my feet. She smiled. I backed away. I was afraid she planned on touching me. If she touched me I couldn't be responsible for my actions because my entire body was an erogenous zone.

"Don't touch me," I said, backing up. I felt the wall behind me and flattened against it.

She touched me. She leaned against me with her whole body and pressed one leg between mine. She was six inches shorter than I was and fifty pounds lighter. In a fair fight I couldn't have beaten the hell out of her.

"Denise," I said, "don't."

Her hand slipped inside my pants and she did something that made my knuckles whiten and my breath stop: She circled her fingers around my manhood. The floor of the pit rushed toward me and I saw the headlights of my life pass in review.

"Are you *sure* you don't wanna?" she said.

10

The Highlights of My Life

The first year

Delivered by Dr. J. Moes, with Nurse K. O'Harran in attendance. Weight: eight pounds. Gifts included six sweaters, seven dresses, four rubber pants, a silk bonnet, a rubber sheet, and ten dollars. Baptized at three weeks by Father Grundy. All facts recorded in *Our Baby's Biography*, illustrated by Mabel Betsy Hill and published by C. R. Gibson and Company, New York. Manufactured in USA. Notations in my mother's hand.

The second year

Began talking, but mostly in cliches.

The third year

No highlights.

The fourth year

First correct use of the subjunctive, more than likely accidental. Earliest memory: sweeping a dozen glass bottles onto the tile floor of the barber shop where my father worked. Began disagreeing, ineptly.

The fifth year

Kindergarten with Sister Mary Jean at the helm, the beginning of my formal education. At recess we went outside to play and after recess we went inside to play. She equipped us with crayons and showed us how to render rolls of butcher paper unfit for further use. We spent half an hour every day memorizing the Our Father, the Hail Mary, and the Glory Be. If there was any time left we worked on the Pledge of Allegiance. Sometimes our door opened and ferocious nuns looked in and smiled.

First grade

A room with rows of wooden chairs in which we had to sit all day.

Second grade

Into the gloomy church we went, a huddled flock of lambs shepherded by Sister Mary Brigid. Father Slattery was waiting for us in the confessional booth between the marble holy-water font and the wire rack of pamphlets. When my turn came I closed the door behind me and knelt in the darkness, waiting for Father to open the sliding panel in the partition that separated us. A ghostly light filtered through the frosted glass of the door. I couldn't hear anything. I waited a long time. The ventilation was poor. Finally the panel opened and a square of dim light appeared in the center of a handkerchief tacked to the wall just above me. I rose half to my feet to bring my face even with it. The shadow I saw through the cloth must have been cast by Father Slattery's head as he leaned forward to hear my confession. I leaned forward, too. We both listened intently. We waited for something to happen, he and I, alone together in the darkness. He asked in a whisper if anybody was there and I said yes and he told me to go ahead.

"Bless me, Father, for I have sinned. This is my first confession and I have committed the following sins: I missed my morning prayers two times and my evening prayers one time and I disobeyed my mother and father two times and I said a bad word one time and I am heartily sorry for having offended God and I promise never to commit them again in the name of the Father, and of the Son, and of the Holy Ghost, amen." I groped for the doorknob, thinking I was finished.

"The bad word," Father whispered, "did it have to do with the body or with taking the name of the Lord thy God in vain?"

I didn't know what to say. Sister Brigid hadn't told us there would be questions.

"Was the word something about your body?"

"Well . . ."

"Just give me a general idea."

I fell silent, blushing.

"Can you spell it?"

"I think so, Father. I think it's f-a-t."

"*Fat? You said fat?*"

"No."

"It's not a sin to say *fat*. You don't have to confess *fat*."

"Not *fat*. F-r-a-t."

"*Frat?*"

"F-a-t-r? F-o-r-t?"

"I see. That's a bodily function. Now, I want you to listen to me. Don't use vulgar words when you talk about your body. Your body is one of God's greatest miracles and it deserves to be treated with reverence. When you receive your first holy communion the body of Jesus Christ Himself will be within you. Your body will be a temple of God. So you must never dishonor it with language of the gutter. For your penance say one Hail Mary and one Our Father. Do you understand?"

"Yes, Father."

"Make a sincere promise not to forget your prayers anymore and not to disobey your parents, who have given you so much. Make a good act of contrition."

He shifted into Latin as I started in on the act of contrition, a prayer I had been drilled on over and over. Before I had progressed very far I saw the shadow of his hand making the sign of the cross over me and I heard him say, "*In nomine patri, et filii, et spiritu sancti, amen.* Go in peace and say a prayer for me." The panel slid shut.

I couldn't remember the last part of the prayer. I tried as hard as I could. Reciting it in class with your friends is a lot easier than doing it alone in the dark when you are face to face with your Maker. Minutes went by. I heard Sister Brigid whispering, "Thomas? Thomas?" I couldn't find the knob.

Suddenly the door swung open. Sister was standing there and she was not happy. "*What is the matter?*" she hissed through clenched teeth.

Tears were in my eyes. "What comes after 'through my most grievous fault'?" I asked.

On Sunday I made my first holy communion. The girls wore white dresses and white shoes and sat on the left side of the church, in front of the statue of the Blessed Virgin Mary. The boys wore white suits and shoes and sat on the right, in front of St. Joseph. We all carried blue prayer books. The church was full of smiling people. As we filed to the communion rail, Mrs. Hofstaeder played something restrained and eerie on the organ. She was not as old as she was to get later. When Father Grundy got to me I tilted back my head and opened my mouth to make it easy for him to put the thin white disc on my tongue, then I bowed my head and closed my eyes for a moment like the others. I rose and returned to my pew, opening my eyes just enough to make sure I didn't step on the heels of the boy in front of me.

I knelt down, full of grace, pure of heart, white of soul, the Holy Eucharist stuck to the roof of my mouth. I worked at it with the tip of my tongue, trying to curl back an edge so I could get under it and pry it off. My friends were having the same trouble, judging from the flickering jaw muscles and Adam's apples. The thing had to be done very carefully because there was a rule against allowing the wafer to touch the teeth, where a piece of it might become lodged and later defiled by contact with Wheaties and chili and so on. At last it became saturated with saliva, relaxed its grip and fell to my tongue, where I was able to wad it into a soggy lump and swallow it.

When Mass was over and the priest and his two altar boys had swept grandly from the altar into the sacristy, the first-communicants rose and filed out of the church in a double file, boys paired with girls, while the organ shook with triumphant military-religious crescendos. Outside, the morning sunlight bouncing off the white clothes was blinding. Grown-ups congratulated us and told us we looked wonderful and cute. Mrs. Hofstaeder's collie bounded across the street and bit me on the wrist.

Question Not Yet Satisfactorily Answered (QNYSA): Why was it wrong to let food touch the Host in the mouth when far worse things were going to happen to it in the stomach?

Third grade

Rose McNerney peed in her pants while sitting in class. A puddle formed under her desk. She sat stiffly, her face a deep red. It took Sister Mary Daniel a long time to figure out what the problem was, even after three different girls explained it to her in whispers. Finally she asked the class to take an unscheduled recess. We filed out, leaving Rose in her seat staring straight ahead. When we came back she was gone and the mess had been mopped up. Rose didn't come back to school until Monday. She spent the rest of the year under a cloud.

On Good Friday, after Holy Thursday, when all the statues in the church were covered with purple shrouds out of respect for Lent, Sister stood before the class holding a small, clear plastic case. In it was a pad of cotton, and on the cotton was a splinter of wood. It was a fragment of the True Cross! Each of us got to hold it for a minute and meditate on its meaning. Almighty God had sent His only begotten Son, Jesus Christ, Our Lord, to earth to redeem mankind through the sacrifice of His life. Jews and Italian soldiers tortured Him and nailed Him to the cross. He died after hanging there from noon until three in the afternoon. He didn't die permanently, of course, being God, rising after three days and ascending into Heaven to rejoin Himself and sit on His own right hand. Before my eyes was a piece of the actual cross on which Our Blessed Redeemer had temporarily died! A relic of unimaginable holiness, once soaked with the Precious Blood of God Himself!

QNYSA: Italians okay, but how could the Jews have done such a thing?

Fourth grade

Billy Phelps, a classmate who was always pale, died. We went as a group to his house, where he was laid out in a small casket surrounded by flowers, his eyes closed and his hands folded on his chest with a rosary. I knelt and gazed at him and said a prayer for the repose of his soul. I felt sad, even though he was never much fun. Mysteriously, he was gone forever. He would never know how anything turned out.

His mother and father had been doing a lot of crying, you could tell. They very much appreciated, they said, that Billy's whole class had come to the wake. Billy loved all of us very much, they said, and would miss us. We said we loved him and would miss him, too. Mr. Phelps said that Billy had had a weak heart that stopped. Apparently when your heart stops, one thing leads to another and you turn into a wax dummy. He told us about being in the hospital room with the doctors and nurses at the end listening to Billy's weak heart rising and falling. When they couldn't hear it any more they knew that God had called Billy back.

I didn't laugh for the rest of the day. That night I told God privately that if he would return Billy I would play with him and be nicer to him. I knew without being told that my request would be turned down.

QNYSA: If God wanted Billy so much, why did he give him to his Mom and Dad in the first place? God should have known they would become attached to him.

Fifth grade

In arithmetic class, after six weeks of steady progress with fractions, Sister Mary Veronica revealed a profound and far-reaching truth: All problems do not necessarily come out even.

My father fulfilled a lifelong ambition. He told his boss, the owner of the barber shop in the Hotel Iowa, to go jump in the lake. He borrowed money and went into the construction business, curbs and gutters a specialty. My mother said she hoped it wasn't a terrible mistake.

Monsignor McCauley died. The tolling of the church bell for two days straight led to a law suit alleging that Catholic funerals were a public nuisance. It was thrown out of court by Judge O'Shaugnessy. The Protestant couple who filed it moved to Chicago, where, rumor had it, they died covered with chancres.

Sixth grade

I got my first erections, casting girls in a new light. Germany invaded Russia. I had a wet dream and then another. Japan attacked Pearl Harbor, the Philippines, and Malaya. I learned the facts of life in the gutter—actually sitting on a curbing with my cousin from Wahpeton, Lester Orfenlech, a high-school freshman. His story seemed incredible at first, but it held together with a terrible logic, and an array of nagging facts suddenly made sense. Women got oddly fat before becoming mothers; girls had a slot between their legs, boys a tab; if the tab didn't get stiff it couldn't be put in the slot; boy dogs climb on girl dogs, animals got milk from their mothers. If I had used my brains I could have put it all together on my own. Because around older guys I always pretended to know more than I did, and because my parents changed the subject whenever I approached it, I had to wait for Lester Orfenlech and a cold curbstone.

That night in bed I couldn't get to sleep. I knew Lester had told me something of extreme importance. I tossed and turned. The door opened and there was my mother silhouetted by the hall light, her face fantastic behind some sort of fluorescent cold cream.

"You were with the Orfenlech boy, weren't you?" she asked sadly.

She not only had an eerie ability to guess the number of beans in a jar, she also could read my mind.

"Yes," I said.

"Did he tell you something?"

"Yes."

I lay still. There was a silence, then my mother said the only thing I ever heard from her about sex.

"Try not to think about it," she said, and closed the door.

The United States landed in Algeria.

QNYSA: If you put the tab in the slot and let yourself go, what was to prevent you from urinating instead of ejaculating?

Seventh grade

I learned how to masturbate. Six of us were on a hike along Catfish Creek, south of town. Hans Kruger was with us. He lived in a house whose front yard featured a refrig-

76

erator and a rusting car chassis. It was Hans who proposed a jacking-off contest. He said he could sit on the ground with his legs out in front of him and shoot over his shoes. We said *he* couldn't, but that *we* could. We pretended to go along with the game, laughing, unbuttoning our flies, and not dreaming that he would go through with it. Quick as a flash he had his thing out and his fist flying. We buttoned up and watched him. He didn't care that he was alone. He liked being the center of attention. True to his word, when he came, several of the white spurts cleared his shoes.

On the way home Hans did most of the laughing and talking. The rest of us were embarrassed by what had happened. I wondered if I should have tried to stop him. What he had done was no doubt a serious sin. I couldn't imagine any of the twelve apostles doing such a thing, with the possible exception of Judas, who would have demanded money.

I tried it myself that night in bed, in my private world of darkness under the covers. I rolled up a bathroom towel and made love to it, pretending it was Deanna Durbin. The pleasure I felt at the climax was immediately invaded by guilt. Within an hour I was on my knees at the side of the bed, apologizing to Deanna and God. Making sure everyone in the house was asleep, I sneaked out of the kitchen door and made my way to a dump several blocks away, where I tried to burn the towel. It sent up a column of smoke but wouldn't catch fire. I finally had to bury it under a pile of rubbish.

Back under the covers I had a nightmare about millions of blind tadpole sperms trapped in that smoldering towel, screaming and choking, groping for a vaginal canal to escape into, finding nothing but tufts of terrycloth wherever they wiggled, suffocating in the end under tons of garbage and trash. Millions of them! The encyclopedia said so! It was staggering to realize that if the war killed every male in the world except me, I could, in a single spasm, repopulate the entire planet, provided that a distribution system could be worked out.

"Where is that green bath towel?" my mother asked a week or so later, going through the house, gathering laundry. "The one with the pretty monogram on it. Have you seen it, Tommy?"

77

"Gee, no, Mom. The green one? Gosh, I don't know where it is."

"Well, that's funny. It can't just have gone up in smoke."

It could have, after having been copulated to death.

QNYSA: Why are sins fun?

Eighth grade

The 1943–44 school year was packed with thrills, not all of them provided by World War II. My debut as an altar boy in the big church was such a flop that I was inducted into Porky Schornhorst's Raiders, the most prestigious gang of troublemakers in town. In the darkness of a winter morning, when I was on my way to serve Mass, I paused to press my nose against Gretchen Schwartz's windowpane and saw the glories of her succulent body. I staggered away with the Washington Monument in my pants, and for years afterward imagined her shinnying up the drainpipe outside my bedroom. If Aristotle, King James, Tchaikovsky, and probably a lot of other people had seen her as I saw her, and at my age, they never would have gone on to become perverts. Sister Raphael, my eighth-grade teacher, picked up a ruler that had inches on one side and centimeters on the other and hit me with it every day from September to June. For sniggering during the Benedicamus, Father Grundy slapped me so hard that my head flew across the room and shattered a blackboard. Hank Clancy chased me onto the third floor rain gutter, where I saw the face of Death. By rescuing me, Sister Mary Jean assured herself a place in heaven. Porky Schornhorst nearly turned himself into Joan of Arc when his attempt to light a fart went awry. After Porky enlisted in the Marines, the Raiders disintegrated and the campaign against the Japanese picked up speed. My jolly older brother Paul returned from the war without one of his feet. As far as I was concerned, God had a lot of explaining to do.

11

Imbroglio in the Seraglio

I was confronted by the Devil himself in the form of a mere slip of a girl, a former student at the University of Colorado, who had me espaliered against a whorehouse wall. Her cool fingers were inside my shorts and around my dinkey, which was getting less dinkey all the time. She could feel the blood pulsing into it and she smiled.

"Denise," I said in a faraway voice, "let me go."

"No," she said. Her friendly squeeze almost made me pass out.

The Rest of the Highlights of My Life:

Freshman year

During a short-lived spate of anticlericalism, my brother Paul urged my parents to send me to high school at Dubuque Central. Not wishing to insult the nuns and priests who had labored over me for so many years, they left me at St. Procopius. Miffed, Paul moved to Chicago and quit six jobs in six months. He came back to Dubuque to mope and sulk. He had lost all traces of his former jollity. He complained of being unable to find a girl, a job, or an artificial foot that felt right. He started hanging around the church a lot.

Germany's defenses collapsed and I felt Helene Hanson's other boob. Her first boob came my way the winter before when the toboggan we were riding turned over and her chest landed on me. Atom bombs blitzed Japan into submission, teaching everybody not to mess with a democracy based on competitive free enterprise and a strong parochial-school system.

Helene's other boob was on her right side, or my left as I faced her. Taken together, her boobs were the most prominent feature of the school and should have been memorialized on the cover of the yearbook. The girls at St. Procopius had to wear blue uniforms with white cuffs and collars, but that didn't make Helene lose her individuality. She stood out in a crowd because it always looked as if somebody was hiding inside her blouse.

We were walking toward each other in a school corridor. She was two years older and naturally treated me as if I were invisible, which enabled me to stare at her openly. One of us tripped and we crashed into each other. I raised my hands reflexively and dropped everything I was carrying. By the sheerest accident, my palm received her breast and stuck there as we fell to the floor in a shower of pencils and books. The softness was a revelation—somewhere I had picked up the idea that breasts put up quite a bit of resistance. I hit the side of my head on the edge of a step, which was a small price to pay for the boon I had been granted by a capricious God. My hand had been engulfed by Helene Hanson's breast without the penalty of sin! She wasn't hurt; she laughed a little, in fact, as she got to her feet. I helped her pick up her books and she said she guessed we should both watch where we were going and she hoped I wasn't hurt. Big boobs hadn't ruined her personality.

She had no idea that I had ravished her upper left side, but I was in a state of shock all day, hardly hearing a word that was spoken to me. The endless softness! I masturbated twice that week, piling one heinous sin on another, and when I confessed them at the end of the month Father Slattery bawled the hell out of me. Unless I conquered the temptations of the flesh at once, he warned, I would likely suffer the tortures of the damned forever. Father Breen came to town not long after and delivered his hair-raising retreat lecture on love and marriage, making me realize just how disgusting my bodily tendencies were. I made up my mind that I would not let all the fine, decent things in my life be poisoned by my natural instincts. I swore off sex.

It wasn't easy. I liked girls. I would have been willing to go all the way with half the female population of St. Procopius. There were seven or eight I couldn't even look at without having vile thoughts to confess. Some of them were deliberate teases—they never exhaled and they writhed when they walked. Others tried to be inconspicuous and not disrupt my train of thought. They failed.

QNYSA: If God was omniscient, as it was widely and confidently assumed, why did he give the Devil an unfair advantage?

Sophomore year

I had a problem. I wanted a date but had lost the nerve to ask anybody. I couldn't even bring myself to ask a girl to the Halloween dance in the church basement when I would be wearing a mask. I was finding it hard to get to know girls as people because of their bodies. I was uncomfortable when alone with a girl because I blushed easily, especially when nothing was said. I couldn't talk about what I was thinking, so I couldn't talk at all. Girls were polite to me, but seemed glad when I went away. I developed acne and decided to become a priest. I only masturbated once during Lent.

Hank Clancy and Porky Schornhorst were discharged from the service and showed up in uniforms covered with ribbons, even though they hadn't killed anybody. Porky had spent his entire hitch on Oahu teaching WACS to play volleyball. I thought maybe he would want to break a few streetlights for old time's sake, but no. All he wanted to do was hang around Bernice Vorwald, onetime Queen of Fat, who had slimmed down during the war because of the shortage of chocolate. Much to my disgust, they got married and immediately had what seemed like seven infant daughters. Hank got a football scholarship to Notre Dame, where he dislocated his hip and met Johnny Lujack. Everybody was changing. The world was changing. I got the uneasy feeling that the good old days were not going to return.

Junior year

More shocks. Gretchen Schwartz showed a suspicious thickening in her midsection. All eyes turned toward the ferretlike older man she was secretly dating, a Lutheran toothpaste salesman from Cuba City, Wisconsin. They got married on All Saints Day and left the Upper Mississippi Valley entirely. I never forgot her.

Paul, who couldn't hold a job but who refused to go to Cedar Rapids to see the psychiatrist, joined a monastic order that allowed the one-footed. Mom cried for a week, even though in a cloister Paul was as close to God as it was possible to get without actually being dead.

I waited for the Call. The Call was a definite sign from God that he wanted you in one of the holy orders. I asked him over and over again during Mass and bedtime prayers what he wanted to do with my life. No answer, no matter how I phrased the question. Several times I got a vague feeling that God was *about* to answer, was maybe *working* on an answer, but nothing eventuated. Gradually girls seemed worthy of further consideration. I got a date for the junior prom, then canceled it because of a pimple on my lip.

Father Breen returned and repeated his sex lecture, gesture for gesture, threat for threat. I was stunned. "Same old bullshit," Hans Kruger said as we filed out of the gym. The rest of the year was filled with questions not yet satisfactorily answered. Of course, they weren't satisfactorily asked, either.

Solid geometry. Acne. Trigonometry. Asthma.

Senior year

It suddenly occurred to me that Joline Breitbach, a sophomore and my next-door neighbor, was a girl. We had been walking to school together for years. I knew her so well I thought of her as a friend instead of as a girl. I don't know when it happened, but one day I became aware of her gender and wanted to engage in sexual congress with her. I found myself thinking of her during every waking moment. Sometimes I woke up in the morning with an erection, proving that I had been thinking of her even while uncon-

82

scious. We started going to movies and parties and novenas together.

One weekend afternoon we were walking along Catfish Creek just below Julien Dubuque's grave. I took her hand and she smiled. We sat on a log and I kissed her right on the middle of the mouth. I had kissed girls before, but that was the first time I ever got it centered on the first try. When the kiss was over she was still smiling, and I never felt so wonderful in all my life. By the time the graduation dance rolled around we had kissed between nine hundred and a thousand times and never got caught once. I didn't touch her boobs. It didn't seem right to touch the boobs of such a fine person.

We went to the dance in grand style, in my family's 1947 Chevrolet with the push-button radio. Afterward we parked next to the Molo Sand and Gravel yard and necked. It was pitch black and we split a bottle of beer. I began to wonder if Joline thought I didn't *want* to touch her boobs, didn't have enough imagination to think of it, didn't like them, was too chickenshit to try, or was queer. So I let my hand slip slowly from her hair to her ear and from her ear to her collarbone. A moment later my hand was lovingly cupped over what turned out to be her corsage. Below her corsage my fingers searched through the endless satin pleats of her formal until they found a wire semicircle, in the center of which was her boob. It may not have matched Helene Hanson's for sheer bulk, but it was more elegantly curved. Besides, Joline was prettier, had better posture, and was at least twice as smart. She got straight A's without half trying. When you touched one of Joline Breitbach's boobs, you were *doing* something.

I purred so she would know how good she felt to me. I would have been happy to leave my hand on her boob for fifty years, to follow her around town, through life, up and down stairs, with my hand on her boob. Clearly I had lost my mind. Joline pushed my hand away and groaned in a way that showed that she was sorry our relationship had taken such an ugly turn. We rolled apart and stared into the fogged windshield, cooling off. I was heartbroken and close to tears. I had lost control of my hands. I had touched her outside of wedlock and without the slightest intention of propagating the species. We both knew what had to be done.

"Tommy, we can't see each other anymore."

"I know."

On her front porch, a last, lingering kiss. I clung to her so desperately that she more or less had to peel me off.

Those priests and nuns knew what they were talking about! Going steady was a ticket to damnation. When a couple reached a stage of easy familiarity, gestures and touches of simple affection could lead to an abuse of body functions that were implanted by God in man to ensure reproduction. In the grip of powerful forces they don't understand, young people can end up engaging in the ultimate act itself merely for the transitory pleasure it affords, which is one of the worst sins imaginable. The act is a solemn ritual designed to reinforce the bonds of marriage and to create a new soul. To think of it as "fun" was contemptible. By seeing so much of each other, Joline and I had challenged impossible odds, and lost. Now, because we held each other in such high esteem—we may even have been in love—we had to break off the relationship to avoid losing our souls. Such thinking was considered rational at the time.

Whenever there was any doubt about what was right and what was wrong, there was a simple test. Would your mother approve? Would you go ahead if she was standing by your side? You didn't have to bring in the Blessed Virgin Mary, Our Holy Mother, Mother of God, Queen of Peace, and Star of the Sea, although she could be resorted to in stubborn cases. Your earthly mother was usually sufficient. Your mother could tolerate watching you kiss your girl good night, but not if heavy breathing was involved. It was an excellent test, capable of fine discrimination. By means of it you could tell exactly how long a good-night kiss could be held without having it change from a sweet expression of affection into something rotten.

At least you could if you imagined *my* mother. It wouldn't work with some mothers. Willie Richards had a gorgeous mother. When she had her hair done she looked like a movie star. We could never figure out why Mr. Richards had left her. He must have been crazy or blind. On New Year's Eve we used to hang around Willie's house, hoping we could kiss his mother at midnight. It happened once. When I was a sophomore she came home early from a party with her makeup streaked by tears. At the stroke of twelve, when the sounds of horns and firecrackers were floating across the town, she came out of her bedroom in silk pajamas and gave us all a kiss on the mouth.

My mother was not like that. She was not what you would call fun. When I was young she was already old, with a lined face that reflected the grief Irish women had suffered down through the ages with drunken husbands. There was no way you could commit a sin or get into any kind of mischief if you imagined her standing next to you.

My mother always had something in her hands that suggested work—a laundry basket, a glob of bread dough, a coal shovel. She had no hobbies. Housework was both her job and her recreation. Sometimes when she looked at me she burst into tears and hugged me, telling me how precious I was to her and leaving hand prints on my shirt in flour or Clorox. Such displays embarrassed me and I always tried to duck out of her grasp.

I guess I was precious to her. She had given birth to two other children and had lost them both, one to scarlet fever and the other to a monastery. My brother Paul was now Brother Pachomius. He was in a deep cloister somewhere in Pennsylvania. He wasn't even supposed to talk, much less write letters or come home once in a while to help clean the cellar or put up the storm windows. Apparently he spent all his time trying to reach a state of total self-abnegation. Every Christmas we got a note in Latin from the abbot implying that Paul was still technically alive. Although my mother was very religious, she had no sympathy for the contemplative orders. Not with so much work to be done.

And what would my mother, born Margaret Loomis in 1890 in Peosta, Iowa, think of me now, spread-eagled against a whorehouse wall, a harlot's arm plunged to the elbow down my pants? Not a pretty sight, was it, Mrs. Shannon? Hardly a just reward for a lifetime of sacrifices. It might have killed her, seeing her son in such a tableau. At the very least she would have screamed, prayed, fainted, and cried. Because she was the way she was, imagining her looking at me disapprovingly gave me the strength I needed to recover control of my life. The blood began to surge *out* of my dinkey.

"What's your trouble, anyway?" asked Denise, withdrawing her arm.

"I want to do it when *I* want to do it," I said, "not when you or Alex want me to do it." Oddly, a few tears came to my eyes.

"What's with him?" said Alex.

"He's hopeless, I told you," said Denise. "He needs to be coaxed. He wants me to talk philosophy with him for a couple of hours first, I think. I don't have the time . . . unless you have the money."

That made me mad. I blew up. "You damned fools!" I shouted. "You don't know the meaning of trust and decency and love and degradation! What would your mothers think of what goes on here? What would God think?" I wanted to go home. I wanted to be with my Mom and Dad.

"Maybe there is no God," Wayne said.

"But if there *is* a God," I said, "what would he think?"

"How the hell should we know?" Alex said. "How can anybody know what a hypothesis thinks?"

"He's *told* you what he thinks," I raved. "In the Bible! All you have to do is open your eyes and read it!"

Archy appeared in the doorway in shirttails, his pants folded over his arm. "If God has some instructions for me," he said, "he's free to call. I'm in the book."

"I hope you enjoy hell," I said, "because that's where you are all headed." I ran down the stairs.

"So that's it," I heard Denise say, "a religious nut! Why didn't somebody tell me? Those guys can be *dangerous*!"

I found the car where it had lurched to the curb and died. Steam was still rising from seams in the hood. From the chaos in the back seat I retrieved my sweater and the paper bag full of my shaving gear, toothbrush, and wash rag. I stuck the road map in my back pocket. Dubuque was only a couple of hundred miles away. With luck I could hitchhike there by nightfall.

Alex and Wayne arrived, puffing after the two-block run.

"I'm hitchhiking home," I announced. "I've been thinking things over and I've come to some conclusions. You wouldn't understand, so don't even try. Just leave me alone."

"Listen, Shannon," Alex said, "It was just a joke. I thought you *wanted* to have some fun and were just kidding about being along for the ride."

"There are some things I don't kid about."

"I should have put a stop to it," Wayne said.

"I don't blame you guys," I said. "You don't know any better. Some day I hope you wake up to the meaning of some of the eternal values."

"Tell me one thing," Alex said. "Do you really believe all that stuff about God and the Bible and the Pope? If I thought you really believed it, I never would have put that broad up to grabbing you by the shmuck."

"Yes, I really believe it." At that moment I believed it more strongly than I ever had. I interpreted my outburst of temper and my churning emotions as a mystical experience.

Alex, his lips tight, shook his head in bafflement. I was a total mystery to him. He started to say something, but couldn't find words.

"Good-bye," I said. "I'll be back at school in a day or two." I turned and walked toward the highway.

Archy came running up, fussing with his fly. "Goddam this zipper! I think she broke it. Shannon! Where the hell are you going? You can't just walk out! What about your share of the gas?"

"Better let him go," Wayne said, putting a hand on his shoulder. "He's throwing some kind of fit."

12

Mom and Dad at Home

A breeder returning from Chicago in an empty pig truck gave me a lift the final fifteen miles from Galena, birthplace of Ulysses S. Grant, to Dubuque, birthplace of Thomas Edward Shannon. Grant's home had been beautifully restored; mine was deteriorating ineluctably. I stood across the street looking at it in the dusk, surrounded by childhood memories. The ambience of the old neighborhood changed with each flash of the traffic lights on the corner. As always, the air carried a hint of the Dubuque Meat Packing Company.

I caressed the rough bark of the tree I was leaning against, which I had climbed many times as a lad. I had, in fact, climbed every tree in a two-block radius of where I stood. I liked climbing trees, not just to see the view and scare my mother, but because I knew it would help make me a success in life. Elbert Hubbard said so. There were five books in our home: a Bible, a missal, a manual of first aid, a 1936 dictionary from which *F-G-H* had been torn by a visiting baby, and *Little Journeys into the Homes of Great Men* by Elbert Hubbard. My father read Hubbard to me when I was small. It was Hubbard who wrote: "Have you ever noticed that a boy who climbs trees usually amounts to something?" My mother said that Elbert Hubbard was a wise and good man, even though he wasn't a Catholic. My father said that Mr. Hubbard had converted to Catholicism on his deathbed, as had practically every other great man worth mentioning, a fact you will never see in any big-city newspaper, interestingly enough.

My mother answered the door. She was holding the garbage pail from under the kitchen sink.

"Tommy! What on earth . . . are you all right?"

"Hi, Mom! Everything's fine! Had a chance to spend one night at home, so I took it. Got to leave bright and early in the morning. Here, let me take that. . . ."

I took the pail from her and carried it through the house and out the back door, explaining as I went that my roommate's car had broken down while we were on a weekend jaunt to visit friends of his and that I had taken the opportunity of hitchhiking home while the car was being fixed. The screen door banged like old times, and my mother peered into the darkness from the kitchen with a worried look on her face, just as I remembered her. I was nearly twenty-one years old and I had been taking out the garbage for seventeen years. One of the reasons I went away to college was to try to reach a higher plateau.

"I hope you aren't making a mistake," my mother said, "coming home like this when you should be studying, riding around at night in old cars with non-Catholics."

"I wasn't with just any old non-Catholics, Mom, I was with my roommates. Archy Nugent is a very good driver and his car never broke down before. Where's Dad?"

Dad was in bed with some sort of flu he couldn't shake. Despite our protests he put on his bathrobe and joined us at the kitchen table. She opened a bottle of beer for him ("to keep him from sneaking something stronger"), heated some coffee for herself, and fixed me some hot cocoa, the kind with the skin on top that she knew I liked. It was good to be home, good to be in a place with familiar smells, with furniture, drapes, and linoleum I had watched grow old. The dining-room rug was threadbare, the radio needed throwing out, and the paint on the kitchen ceiling had begun to peel and flake. There were a lot of things they could have bought with the money it was costing them to put me through college, and every once in a while I appreciated what they were doing for me.

Shabbiness could be seen in the house, but not dirt. Dirt could never establish a foothold because it had my mother to content with. She was a housekeeper in the heroic tradition—tireless, maniacal, superhumanly strong. Dirt was anathema, and the daylight hours were spent in a relentless crusade against it. She often strode into battle before the sun rose, armed with dustpans, mops, brooms, and buckets. When the going got rough and the danger arose that dirt might carry the day, she resorted to chemical warfare with such weapons as ammonia, Drano, and homemade soap. My father and I never had to set an alarm—when it was time for us to get up my mother simply lowered her restraints and allowed the natural clang and thump of the battle to wake us.

It was no good to help her with her chores or tell her not to work so hard. She was least unhappy when she had some thankless job to do and little prospect of getting it done before something else had to be started. It was better to humor her, Dad and I agreed. Let her do whatever she wanted. She liked to work? Then *let* her, for heaven's sake! Don't take her one pleasure from her.

If Dad had won the Irish Sweepstakes, propelling us into a life of ease where the cooking, cleaning, laundry, and worrying could have been hired out to a Swedish couple, my mother would have been stripped of her sense of mission and would have disintegrated.

Not that my father would have bought a winning sweepstakes ticket. He was not the lucky type. He was not the gambling type, either, fortunately. He had taken only two chances in his life and those were enough. Quitting his job as a salaried barber to start a construction company, then abandoning that and plunging into debt to open his own shop was the last gambling he would ever do.

Shannon's Barber Shop was a flop by every rational standard of accounting. It stayed afloat on zeal alone. Hung over or not, Dad opened the place at six thirty in the morning to catch the early trade and stayed open till seven at night, working himself to near exhaustion daily in an effort to be a success as an independent businessman. Several times the Hotel Iowa asked him to come back, but to accept even the first chair would have smacked of defeat, if not ignominy.

He talked less and less of the chain of luxury tonsorial salons he planned to open in Cascade, Peosta, Dickeyville,

Hazel Green, and "maybe on into Madison." Now he didn't even try to keep all of his four chairs staffed. Often he worked alone. Turnover among his assistant barbers was high. They weren't willing to work for low pay simply for the chance of getting in on the ground floor of the proposed chain, and they tired of his line of chatter. He talked incessantly, which had a soothing effect on the customers while leading the other barbers to seek employment elsewhere. Only Felix Kolmorgan stayed with him year after year, manning Chair Number Two on busy afternoons. Felix was hard of hearing.

My mother served as manicurist for a while. She didn't work out, not just because she wasn't a sex symbol, but because she couldn't relax, which made everybody else tense, too. She would lay down a half-completed thumb and stare into space until Dad cleared his throat. He and I knew what was distracting her. She was thinking of rugs at home that could be vacuumed, of steadily dimming windows, of dust accumulating unopposed atop moldings and behind the refrigerator. She was too gloomy to be a manicurist, that's what it came down to. She had a habit of shaking her head sadly when everyone else was laughing at a customer's joke.

My mother was physically indestructible; years of drinking and overwork were wrecking my father. In his younger days, according to browned photographs and my own faint memory, he was flagpole straight and bright-eyed, his wavy, reddish hair a splendid advertisement for his profession. Now he was both balding and fattening, as he put it himself. His face had taken on a sagging, defeated cast. His smile, once so consistent with his personality, now gave the impression of going against the grain. His nose, long dormant, had begun to fill out and change color.

These were my parents. I had come home to tell them that they could count on me, that I wouldn't let them down. I had left Springfield intending to tell them that my Catholic faith had been severely tested by being brought into contact with unbelievers for the first time in my life, but that it had survived and was stronger than ever. That very day I meant to tell them that my faith, showing signs of weakness, had been annealed, case-hardened, and cauterized in a fiery crucible, the nature of which, they should forgive me, I couldn't vouchsafe. I was even prepared to admit that I had deliberately skipped Mass and eaten a hamburger on Friday, but that such things were behind me. They could quit worrying about me and redirect their prayers toward someone who needed them.

As I readied myself to make this confession as we sat around the kitchen table with our coffee, beer, and cocoa, the awareness grew within me that it was already too late. Doubt had stolen up on me again. The rock-ribbed fortress of faith I thought had been newly constructed in my soul had vanished without a whisper. It had been a mirage. I had been pushed to the edge of the abyss in Springfield, and in fear I had wrapped myself in a cloak of faith that had melted away as if it never existed. I had been kidding myself. God, sin, heaven, the whole religious way of looking at life—I simply felt outside of it. I no longer believed. That was it in a nutshell. Years of *trying* to believe hadn't worked. I had gone over the edge, and the abyss was now beneath me.

13

Faith Steps Out

In a sense I had passed the whorehouse sex test I had set
for myself. A human person of the female configuration
had put her adorable little hand inside my shorts and given
my hanging shlong a loving squeeze. I hadn't crumpled and
blubbered and made a fool of myself. No, I had maintained
my self-respect. When it happened I thought the willpower
I had shown derived from some undiscovered river of religious faith within me, and the episode gave me a wonderful sense of elation. I felt a rush of certainty that lasted
nearly an hour. I would no longer be plagued by doubts, I
thought. It was the overall picture that counted and not the
details, just as Father Slattery said. Sure there were a few
nagging discrepancies, but they were the bath water and
not the baby.

I had hitchhiked home to tell my parents that my faith
was impregnable and that as a result my grades were sure
to improve. My mother had always seemed to suspect that
I was not a comfortable believer and that I might backslide
if she didn't keep the pressure on. Why she suspected I
don't know, but as I sat at our kitchen table and looked
into her face, so full of love and worry, I knew that her
fears were richly justified.

"Tommy," she asked unerringly, "are you friendly with
God?"

Dad groaned. "Can't we have a nice little talk without

getting serious?" He pulled his bathrobe more tightly around him.

"Well," my mother sighed, "you know what Father Slattery said in his note."

"What did Father Slattery say?" I asked with sudden alarm. If that son of a bitch had—

"He said you had a nice talk and you worked out some problems."

"Problems? He said *problems*?"

"Yes, but he didn't say what they were."

Dad shifted his feet. "All first-year students at big schools have problems," he said. "Let the kid enjoy his few hours at home."

"If he has problems," Mom said, "he can always bring them to us. We are only as far away as his mailbox. He sends his laundry, why not his problems?"

"It was just stuff having to do with school," I said.

I intended to tell them everything except about the trip to the whorehouse, which I could never have made them understand. Now I could tell them nothing without lying. I searched myself and couldn't find a shred of faith. The realization came to me that the strength I showed in resisting Denise flowed not from a pool of religious conviction but rather from a refusal to be Alex Gold's puppet. Fear no doubt played a part, too—not so much a fear of God as a fear of the clap. I tried to change the subject. It was bewildering: At some point between taking out the garbage and drinking my cocoa I had become a non-Catholic.

"Well, are you?" Mom persisted.

"Can't you let him alone?" Dad said, but weakly.

"Am I what?"

"Friendly with God."

"Gee whiz, Mom, how am I supposed to answer that? By saying that we double-date together?"

"That's not such a crazy way of looking at it. You know what I mean. Do you go to Mass on Sunday?"

"Of *course* I go to Mass on Sunday. . . ."

"And communion?"

"Yes!"

"Do you pray for God's help with these *problems,* whatever they are?"

"Yes, yes, yes!"

I was lying all over the place, but so what? A few minutes earlier, just after leaving the Church, I had become an agnostic.

"Well, I just hope this going away to college wasn't a terrible mistake. You could have stayed at Crown of Thorns and lived right here at home. They are some *very fine* teachers, you know very well. Look at Father Theobald. You would have to go an awful long way to find somebody better than Father Theobald."

"In canon law, sure," I said, "but not in sanitary engineering."

"When I think of the money we would save if you lived at home . . ."

My father drained his glass of beer and slid it across the table to Mom so she could put it in the sink. "He might be coming home whether he wants to or not," he said, "unless his grades improve."

Iowa State, as a matter of policy, sent carbons of report cards to parents. My mother brightened a little at the thought that I might flunk out.

"That's one of the reasons I made this visit," I said, "to tell you not to worry about my grades. They'll get better now that I have . . . cleared some things up in my mind. I'll admit it, I was a little mixed up in the first quarter. I've settled down now. You'll see."

I almost said I had figured everything out just a few minutes earlier, but that would have made my argument sound superficial and not the inevitable culmination of a long process of logical analysis.

"You've got to hit those books, son!" Dad said with as much strength as his flu would allow. "Hit 'em hard!"

"Don't worry, I will."

"No sense overdoing it, though," Mom said, "like your father does night after night at the Legion with that stinking Arnold Gertz, who should be taken to the dump and shot. After all, you aren't well. You have your bronchial tube to worry about."

"You can be half dead and get straight A's," Dad said.

I helped Mom put Dad to bed. "Look at FDR," he went on. "Confined to a wheelchair and president of the United States!"

"I know, Dad. Tomorrow I start hitting the books."

"Not only that," he said, "but you aren't even sick. You're as strong as an ox. Okay, so once in awhile you wheeze. You call that sick? I don't call that sick."

"It could get worse," my mother said.

They were badgering me in their own ways. I couldn't get mad at them. They wanted what was best for me. They loved me. With Paul lost in a cloister, I was more or less their only child. I was their main hope for pride in their old age and for financial security in case the bottom fell out of barbering. If I could land a job with a top-notch treatment plant I could pay them back for all they had done for me. I looked at them. My mother smiled wanly, as if she was the one who was sick. My father winked and gave me a "you can do it" nod. How could I tell them that I had left the Church? I couldn't. I vowed I would never hurt them in that way.

In my old room Mom turned down the blankets and plumped the pillow. "Maybe you should take some time off," she suggested. "Stay here for a week or two and catch your breath. Then go back to Ames and see how your strength is."

"Mom, will you quit treating me like an invalid? Dad's right: I'm as strong as an ox. A tall, thin ox with a bit of asthma. Just because I'm allergic to fuchsias doesn't mean there is anything wrong with my health. I'm leaving for school in the morning. Second-quarter finals are coming up and I've got to start cramming. Please, no more about my health."

We embraced and said good night with tears in our eyes.

Cramming, that was only one thing I wanted to do in the coming week. Another was to go to the library and find out if any famous decent people had ever gone from Catholicism to agnosticism. And I had to find a girl. I had to get this virginity thing behind me once and for all. I didn't want to be the only virgin agnostic in North America.

14

Lucky Lohrke's Sewage Test

Rain sometimes sweeps across Iowa like a wet mop. You can see it coming for miles. On the horizon there is a pile of black-and-white thunderheads, and hanging from them is a gray wall of rain, shimmering and undulating in slow motion. If the breeze is in your face you have only minutes to take cover, unless you want to get soaked. No force on earth can halt the advance of that wet, silvery curtain, not a string of atom bombs, not the shaking of a thousand defiant fists, not the prayers of all the faithful, living and dead.

Second-quarter finals were like that. I knew they were coming. I could almost see them coming in a physical way, as I might have seen the charge of a crazed rhinocerous. Exams are coming, I kept telling myself. I've got to start cramming, got to make up for lost time. I was preoccupied with a number of important matters of a personal nature, but I never should have let so many days slip by. When the first exam struck I had only begun to cram.

I sat in Lucky Lohrke's sewage class and took the consequences. "Lucky," we called him, after the New York Giant infielder of the same name. He walked slowly up and down the aisles, handing out his mimeographed sheets of questions, a faint sadistic smile on his lips. He was a dried-up old man with all the mercy wrung out of him. His skin was patterned like a sunbaked mudflat. His thatch of graying blond hair was matted and askew. He laid a sheet on my desk as he might have laid my neck on a chopping block.

Our eyes met as he passed. It's all over now, Shannon, I knew he was thinking. You are going to pay now for your daydreaming and for your wretched and indecipherable assignments. Remember all those times I called on you and you said you weren't prepared? When you took wild, ignorant guesses? I remember them well. Now I am going to give you what you deserve. I am going to make sure that the American sewage industry never has you around to make things worse. The piece of paper I have put on your desk has questions on it. You won't be able to answer them to my satisfaction. You will flunk the test, Shannon, just as surely as sedimentation follows flocculation. You will flunk the course and, more than likely, flunk out of school as well, and I will never have to look upon your pimply face again.

Oh, yeah? Maybe I would fool old Lucky Lohrke. Maybe by some fluke the test would touch only on those few points with which I was halfway conversant.

1. How is the formula for dissolved oxygen sag

   $$D_t = \frac{K_1 L}{K_2 - K_1}(10^{-k_1 t_1} - 10^{-k_2 t}) + D \times 10^{-k_2 t}$$

   derived from the equations for deoxygenation and atmospheric reaeration, and how it is applied in practice?

2. For raw sewage without buoyant solids, give the formula that shows the logarithmic relationship between disinfectant and bacteria.

The dirty bastard! I thought the questions would be general—the role of sewage treatment down through the ages and in modern civilization, that sort of thing—I didn't think he'd ask about the *mathematics*. I was so pressed for time all quarter that I skipped the formulas entirely, sticking to the big picture, the *romance* of the subject.

I laid my pencil down and covered my eyes with my hands. There I was, an atheist, without a single god to pray to for help. If I were an agnostic, as I had been up until a few days previously, I might have tried praying to somebody, anybody, on the off chance that there was an entity

98

in the cosmos that had some sympathy for the human condition and would be willing to lend a guy a hand. An agnostic, technically, believes that the question of God's existence is unanswerable, that there is no way of knowing whether there is a God, and that it is unwarranted and untenable to hold that there is or isn't. Not only is the evidence insufficient for a conclusion, it must always be insufficient, by the nature of the question. An agnostic, therefore, could launch a prayer born of panic, it seemed to me, without violating any principles, provided he did it in private and provided the situation was desperate, as it was now.

On Tuesday I had abandoned the philosophical stance of agnosticism on the grounds that it was chickenshit. Either God exists or he doesn't, and a person ought to have enough guts to decide one way or the other. I didn't want to go through life with a weltanschauung based on hedging. There are lots of things in life that have to be decided without absolute proof. If we always hang back waiting for every last fact to come in, very little would get done. All right, so I can't prove there is no God. So what? That doesn't prove there is one. Better to take a stand, for Christ's sake.

3. Discuss what was learned in Plainfield, New Jersey, with regard to the amelioration of odors in crude sewage by treatment with chlorine in advance of the Imhoff tanks.

I could do something with that question. I had read the Plainfield case several times. It was a satisfying example of how a community beset by a shared problem had turned to sanitary engineers for relief. The engineers had rolled up their sleeves and plunged in, so to speak, and after they had expended a tremendous amount of brainpower the air above Plainfield was fresh and clean again.

Not that I was completely flummoxed by the math questions. The one about the formula for dissolved oxygen sag wasn't so tough. I could have derived it from the other two in elegant fashion had I bothered to study the section when it was assigned. I just couldn't imagine anybody being a big enough turd to ask it on an exam.

The thing I liked about math was the *precision* of it, the *definiteness* of it. When you worked a problem it was either right or wrong, and when it was right it was exactly right. If x plus y was nine and x minus y was three, then x had to be six and y had to be three. There were no *if*'s, *and*'s, or *but*'s about it. You didn't have to go back and see what Saint Jerome or Pope Innocent VI had to say.

Not so with the theological problems I had been grappling with. In matters of faith and morals everything was spongy, amorphous, impalpable, foggy. What is the soul? Purgatory? The Holy Ghost? Original Sin? Sin? What did Emmanuel Swedenborg mean, exactly? What the hell is the point of the Book of Revelation? You can drive yourself nuts trying to pin down answers to questions like these. I was *so happy* to be rid of them, so *proud* of finding the courage to throw them out. At first I felt a void deep within me, but quite soon I came to perceive it as serenity—a clear, cool, liquid globe of tranquility that was growing, growing. Peace and conviction were spreading over my torso and extremities and sooner or later would reach my outermost nerve endings. When that happened I would be at rest with myself at last, able to concentrate and live up to my early academic promise. I wouldn't be so nervous and jumpy. I would be a finer human being and roommate.

One of the first things I had done upon returning to Ames from Dubuque was to take back to the library all of the books I had borrowed on Catholicism. The librarian remembered me. I had been in several times to replenish my stock.

"That must be some paper you are writing," she said. "I don't think I've ever seen an undergraduate do so much research."

"It's done," I said. "I got an *A*. Now I have another assignment. I have to write a paper on how I would persuade a Martian *not* to become a Catholic."

"*Not* to become a Catholic?"

"I have to show that Catholicism is the *last* religion a Martian in his right mind should join."

"I see."

"So what have you got attacking Catholics?"

She frowned thoughtfully.

"It doesn't have to attack Catholics only," I added. "Attacks on religion in general would be fine, too. How silly it is and so on."

"Hmm. Yes. Rationalism and free thought are what you want. I'm afraid we're a little spotty in those areas."

She found a few things. I left with *The Decline and Fall of the Roman Empire* by Edward Gibbon, *Greatest Lectures* by Robert G. Ingersoll, *The Age of Reason* by Thomas Paine, a brand-new one called *Man and His Gods* by Homer W. Smith, and a pamphlet entitled *So You Want to Be an Atheist!* by Judith Fennimore Montalvo.

4. You have been given the job of designing a treatment plant for an unsewered community of 100,000, liquid wastes from which presently debouch into a river via a trapezoidal ditch. Assume a standard mix of agricultural, domestic, industrial, and institutional sewage. What size plant and what equipment would be required for primary, secondary, and tertiary treatment? What, roughly, would be the chemical composition of the effluent?

It always struck me as odd that for the purposes of sewage treatment that churches were considered institutional. Aside from intellectual garbage, what comes from a church? Every one has a toilet, but toilets, to my mind, should be classified under domestic. What was in churchly effluent that wasn't in domestic? If there were a lot of nuns around, I guess you would find wool lint and maybe starch. Domestic sewage was divided into kitchen and bathroom. Most people are surprised to learn your kitchen wastes, your soaps and greases, are by far the harder of the two to handle at the plant. Not that bathroom wastes are any picnic.

"Time's up!"

What?

"Time's up." It was Lohrke. "Stop writing! Stop writing!"

Good God, time couldn't be up already! I hadn't even gotten started!

Professor Lohrke sped around the room with amazing agility for a man his age, scooping up the papers and wishing the class the best of luck in the future. This was terrible! I had failed the test! I would be kicked out of school!

"Sir, I didn't finish the test," I said to him when the room had cleared. My heart was fluttering wildly and my voice was unsteady.

"Of course you didn't finish it," he said, stuffing papers into a briefcase. "You spent the whole two hours staring out the window."

"I did? I've been having some, well, personal problems, I haven't been able to concentrate lately. If I could take your test again—say in a week or two—I'm sure I could do well on it. All I need is some time to study."

"No."

"Professor Lohrke! You've got to give me another chance!"

He looked at me squarely. "Mr. Shannon, permit me to give you a piece of advice. I've watched you more closely than you might think during the past few months. I've noticed that you have a remarkable gift. You can stare out a window for amazing lengths of time without fatigue or boredom. Give up your dream of being a sanitary engineer. Get a job in a national forest lookout tower watching for fires. You would be good at it and you would be performing a valuable service. Good-bye."

Not good-bye and good luck. Just good-bye.

15

The Sandwiches of Dr. Kellman

Maybe I was in the wrong field. I never dreamed as a child of being a sanitary engineer. Maybe there was a subject I could major in that would keep my attention from wandering off to side issues like eternity and sex. An article in the campus newspaper urged floundering students to see their faculty advisers, who doubled as career-guidance counselors, and take a battery of occupational interest tests administered for a small fee by the Department of Psychology. A feature of the counseling program this year, the article said, was that faculty members were assigned from outside the students' field of interest. That way a fresh point of view could be brought to bear.

It took me six phone calls to find out who my faculty adviser was: Ernest Kellman, Ph.D., Professor Emeritus of Culinary Arts, Department of Home Economics, Room 217, Old Main. I didn't know that the term *emeritus* simply meant that he was retired; I thought he had received certain honors or was in some way especially distinguished. He certainly looked distinguished—an erect man with a full head of white hair and pale blue eyes that seemed to be windows to an endless fund of tested facts. His office was in an aged stone structure wrapped in a heavy blanket of ivy. It seemed to be deserted. The hallways were dark and littered with pieces of glass and plaster. I found Professor Kellman on the second floor, jotting in a notebook, sitting at a desk that was covered with sandwiches, each with one bite taken out of it. As I stood in the doorway he looked at me with an expression of friendly curiosity. I liked his face.

"Excuse me, sir, I don't want to interrupt your lunch. Would you rather I came back another time?"

"Come in, come in. Have a chair. This isn't my lunch. This is a program of ongoing research."

I sat down. He handed me a sandwich.

"Here," he said, "take a bite, about the same size as mine. Include a little of the crust. Wait a minute! Is your mouth full of gum and tobacco and beer and junk like that?"

I assured him that it wasn't.

"Go ahead, then. Good. Now, give me your opinion of the flavor, aroma, freshness, and texture. Use a scale from one to ten, with one delicious and ten vomiting. Fine. Got it? What do you say? Three across the board? Okay. . . ." He entered a three in each of four columns on a sheet labeled SANDWICH A: PEANUT BUTTER. "All right, go on to B. That's jelly. C is jam, D is honey, E is cinnamon, and F is sweet creamery butter sprinkled with granulated sugar."

I did as I was told. My estimates fell generally between two and five.

"Next week I'm going to take up the combinations," he explained while I chewed thoughtfully. "Peanut butter and jelly, cinnamon and sugar, and so on down the line. After that will come the lunch meats and then I'll get into changing the breads. Man, I'll have a hell of a chart when I get through."

"Is this something you're doing for a class, or on a grant, or what?" I took a napkin from a dispenser and touched my lips.

"No, no, no, this is just to kill time. It's completely silly. Of course, I might be able to get a book out of it some day, so it won't be a total waste. Most of my career I taught advanced cookery—the gourmet stuff, French and Chinese and whatnot. What did the milkmaids in my classes care about that? How to get the lumps out of mashed potatoes and gravy, that's all they'll ever have to know. So now that I've got the time I thought I'd look into something simple. Like the great American sandwich. They can't kick me out

104

of here if I keep a project going, see what I mean? There would be too big an outcry. 'Interrupting vital research.' Who would have the nerve to say that it's silly? I was once head of the whole department."

"I don't think it's silly," I said. "There must be a lot of variables and unknowns in sandwiches that nobody has ever investigated."

"For good reason. What difference does it make? No, I'm just fooling around, keeping my hands busy. Can't read much anymore, my eyes get tired. From noon till two I listen to that kook disc jockey on KPIG—his show is mostly quotations on pork bellies and hog futures, but in between he plays harpsichord music. Years ago I was quite the harpsichord fan. Even built one. Still have it down in the cellar someplace."

"Your students might be interested. Students eat a lot of sandwiches."

"I don't have any students! Don't you read the newspapers? I was put on the shelf four years ago! They won't let me near a classroom. They haven't got the guts, though, to throw me out of my office. I've been here since 1913. This is one of the original buildings, did you know that? Put up in 1869 by stonemasons brought over from Italy. Now they want to tear it down for a new wing on Animal Husbandry. How do you like that? What's the good of more pigs and sheep if nobody knows how to cook them?"

"I haven't been keeping up with the local news. I've been having so many problems of my own I hardly know what's going on around me. That's why I came to see you. Are you the last one here? I didn't see anybody else when I came in."

"Been alone now for ten months. They turned the lights and water off once, but I raised such hell they turned them back on. They can't stand the publicity. I'm lovable old Professor Kellman—I've got 'em over a barrel. I sit right here from dawn to dusk, fooling around with my sandwiches. Before that it was different kinds of soda pop. If I didn't show up bright and early they'd bring in a wrecking ball and bash this building to the ground so fast you wouldn't know what hit you."

"You're here every day?"

"Including weekends. They're trying to wait me out. I'm

very good at waiting. You know what they are doing now? Stopping all maintenance. Hoping the place will gradually collapse on me." He reached behind him and threw open some drapes. The window was dark. "Look at that! Solid ivy! Hasn't been cut back since June! Can't tell if it's day or night. If I open the window the vines try to get in. Sometimes I have to beat them back with a broom. In another year the building will be completely covered. Walking by outside, you won't be able to see the place at all. You'll have to be Tarzan to find the door." He laughed cheerfully, then grew serious. "You a reporter? A cop?"

"No, I'm here to talk over my career problems. You're my faculty adviser."

He looked at me blankly.

"You're my career-guidance counselor. I got your name from the student services office. You're supposed to give me advice, the benefit of your experience, and so on."

He lifted his eyebrows. "Is that what they're going to do? Give my name to nine thousand students and have them all troop in here with their goofy problems?"

"If that's what you feel, I might as well leave right now."

"I didn't mean you, I meant *them*. You're probably all right. You broke up my day . . . you helped me with my research. You made a 'significant contribution,' as they put it in the pedagogical journals. Have you ever read a pedagogical journal? You wouldn't believe it. So what's on your mind? I'll give you whatever help I can." He laced his fingers and looked at me with friendly interest.

"It has to do with wondering if I am in my major because I want to be or because my father wants me to be."

"Hm. Is your father smart or dumb?"

"He's a barber, but he's pretty smart. He put me into sanitary engineering. It's a growing field and I'll never have to worry about a job. He's right on that, I'm sure."

"Hold your horses. *Sanitary* engineering? What does that consist of?"

"Solid waste disposal, sewage, sewage treatment, sewerage design . . ."

"They teach that here? At Iowa State?"

"Oh, yes, sir."

"Actual courses on sewers?"

"Yes, sir. It's a big field. Part of civil engineering. You have to know hydraulics, chemistry, city planning, structural analysis and design, all sorts of things."

He leaned back in his chair and whistled. "Why anybody would want to study that is beyond me. Maybe your father is not as smart as you think he is. Sounds to me like he has a problem of some kind. My God, when I flush a toilet I want to *forget* about it."

"Bathroom wastes are just a small part. You soon get so you don't think about them. Sewage comes to a matter of organic chemistry, that's all. It's nice for you to be able to flush a toilet and forget about it—you can thank sanitary engineers for the freedom you have to do that. At the point of the flush, they take over. A whole network of buried pipes is involved. The slopes have to be calculated: too flat and the sewage clogs, too steep and scouring action wears the pipes out. Gravity flow is what you are after because pumping costs money. You have to do some pumping in a town like Ames, it's so flat. The slope of the pipe takes it deeper and deeper until trenching costs go out of sight, then you put in a pump and send the sewage back up to near the surface. You keep going like that till you reach the treatment plant."

"This is all news to me. Could they cut off my sewage the way they did my water? Make everything back up into my sandwiches?"

"They wouldn't dare because of the public health hazard. Let me finish my thought about the pipes. If a gravity conduit is below the water table, quite often the pressure outside is greater than inside, so if the joints leak the flow goes *into* the pipe. When you are pumping sewage uphill you need what we call a pressure pipe. Leaky joints there mean that sewage might seep *out of* the pipe and percolate into the drinking water supply, and you don't want that."

"I'll say not!"

"There is a lot to it, is what I'm trying to say."

"Wonderful. Be a sanitary engineer, then, if that's what you want and your old man can afford it and it doesn't hurt anybody."

"My grades have been terrible. I might flunk out."

He pondered that for a moment, then raised a finger.

"Maybe you're the dumb one, ever thought of that?

107

Maybe you just don't have what it takes. It's nothing to be ashamed of. If you like sewers so much you could try to get a job airing them out or some damned thing."

"I'm pretty good at math. I think I should stay in the technical area."

"You know math? Here's a problem for you. If you had ten different sandwiches and you wanted to combine the fillings in every possible way, how many sandwiches would you be contending with?"

"That's easy. Permutations and combinations. Can I write on the blackboard? Look, you let N equal the number of sandwiches and r the number of fillings you want to put together. If you take fillings two at a time, then r equals 2. Here's the formula:

$$\frac{N!}{(N-r)!}$$

The exclamation mark is no joke—it's called a factorial and it tells you to multiply the number in a descending series. In your problem, putting in the numbers, you have:

$$\frac{10 \times 9 \times 8 \times 7 \times 6 \times 5 \times 4 \times 3 \times 2 \times 1}{8 \times 7 \times 6 \times 5 \times 4 \times 3 \times 2 \times 1}$$

It's easy to figure the answer because most everything cancels out, leaving you with 9 times 10. You end up with 90 sandwiches."

"Ninety! Holy God, I can keep this sandwich thing going for months!"

"You have to define sandwich, though. Say you put jelly on top of the peanut butter. That's one. You could also put the peanut butter on top of the jelly. Do you want to consider that another sandwich?"

"I'd have to call that the same one. Turn it upside down and it would be like spreading the jelly first."

"Okay. Then you have to divide the answer by $r!$, or 2 times 1, which cuts it to 45. That's still a lot of sandwiches."

"Have you ever tried to spread peanut butter on jelly? It can't be done. Every female in the world has learned that through experience."

"You could deduce it from pure physics. The coefficient of friction is so low for jelly it could never overcome the force of adhesion between the peanut butter and the knife."

"You should stay in the sciences."

"I think so, too, but I can't keep my mind on it. I've been spending a lot of time lately losing my religion. I keep going to the library to look things up, to make sure I'm doing the right thing, to pile up facts I can use if I ever have to justify myself to my family and relatives."

"Do you enjoy it? Looking things up? Maybe you could get a job like that. Doing research in libraries for people."

"I don't think the money would be very good."

"No, I guess it wouldn't."

"Sanitary engineering is probably the place for me. I like it. If I could only make myself study. I could if I had a girl friend, I think. The way it is now, when I'm not preparing myself for arguments about religion, I'm thinking about girls."

"Then get into the culinary arts, my boy! The classes are full of girls! You could take your pick. That's what I did. I married a student of mine the first year I taught, one a little on the thin side. With the proper diet I fattened her up until she looked like Miss Iowa. She's still a knockout and she's sixty-five years old."

"I'll think about it. Well, I have to go. I have a class in ten minutes."

"So what are you going to do about your career?"

"Stay put, I guess. I can't think of anything better."

"A wise decision. That's how I see it, anyhow." He rose and shook my hand vigorously. "Thanks for stopping by . . . it was a real pleasure. Take some of these sandwiches with you, I've got plenty. Let me know if there is ever anything I can do for you."

"Thank you, Professor, I'll remember that."

16

How to Find Sex

Dinnertime in the basement of Mrs. Lurella Parkhurst's bungalow. It was Wayne's turn to cook and we were enjoying his specialty—beans and franks with plenty of ketchup. Relations between us had been a bit strained since I walked out on them in Springfield, and the conversation was progressing fitfully. Alex, normally so brash and inconsiderate, seemed affected most. He had hardly said ten words to me since we got back, and now he was playing with his food, plowing pathways through the beans with his fork. After some minutes of this he laid his silverware down, looked at me, and made an unexpected apology.

"I've been thinking things over—the hard time I've been giving you and the whorehouse and so on. As Wayne said, you are entitled to your religion. At the whorehouse, well, I went too far and I'm sorry. Remember the last thing you said to me? You told me you really believed it, the Catholic stuff, and I said I wouldn't get on your back anymore. I mean it. If anybody bothers you . . . just tell me and I'll knock his teeth out. Understand? You just tell me."

It was a hard speech for him to make, and when he was through he shoveled food into his mouth with great energy. Never before had he said anything to me that I was certain was completely sincere, and I reddened. Wayne and Archy looked at their plates in embarrassment.

"Thanks," I said. It was all I could think of. I didn't

know how to cope with sincerity. There was a lingering silence. I would have to bring everybody up to date on my personal philosophy, now that the subject had been raised.

"Alex, I really appreciate that," I said. He shrugged me off with a wave of his fork. "But I have to make a confession. I don't believe it."

"You don't believe I would help you out and stick up for you?"

"No, I don't believe the religious stuff anymore."

They stopped eating and stared at me.

"It strikes me as nonsensical now," I said. "I don't know why it took me so long to see the light."

"When did you decide all this," Archy asked, "this morning?"

"Hell, no . . . it was *days* ago. I've had serious doubts for years."

"What serious doubts?" Alex asked. "You never said anything about serious doubts. You told us what a big believer you were and what sinners we were."

"It was the *way* you attacked the Church that made me defend it. You were hitting below the belt and you didn't know what you were talking about. Well, you were right about one thing—the Vatican pornography. I found out that there is some, but that it's just part of a collection of books that have been banned over the centuries. It's under lock and key and nobody can get in to see it. I don't know why I fought with you the way I did . . . maybe to convince *myself* that I was right. I always wished afterward that I had been on your side of the argument. Springfield was just stupid. Everything came together and I lost my head and blew up and I'd like to forget it."

"This isn't healthy," Wayne said. "A sudden flip-flop. You could have a nervous breakdown. Run amok."

"It's not a sudden flip-flop. Only my announcement is sudden."

"You could set fire to a sofa," Wayne said. "Molest a nun."

"My new position is the result of a long, slow process of reorientation. I've been putting my faith to the test for months. Actual experiments. Why, just two weeks ago I skipped Mass to see if it would make me feel guilty."

"Wait a minute," Alex said. "Two weeks ago? You're

full of crap. You went to Mass. I remember when you went out the door. You said you were going to Mass and I told you to pray for nookie."

"That's where you're wrong," I said triumphantly. "I never said I was going to Mass. I said good-bye, yes. I left a few minutes before Mass started *as if* I were going, but I didn't *say* I was going to Mass. Thinking that I actually went to Mass was an erroneous assumption on your part."

"*Oy gevalt!* The erroneous assumption is that anybody gives a damn!"

"I even left my missal on the desk to prove I had no intention of going. If I go to hell I don't want it to be because I'm a sneak."

"Even the God of the Old Testament wouldn't send a man to hell for being a sneak," said Wayne.

"But he would for being a goddam idiot," Alex said. "Shannon, you're doomed."

Archy proposed that we celebrate my hard-won apostasy by opening a quart of beer. The motion was seconded by Wayne and carried by acclamation. They all assured me that there would be another party when I lost my cherry.

Losing one's cherry at Iowa State College was tremendously difficult in the 1950's. Women were outnumbered by men by more than two to one, and most of those milk-fed farm studs were *big*. Whenever I saw a female with whom I would have been pleased to become familiar, she was almost always under escort by at least one hulking oaf. I felt like asking them why they didn't pick on somebody their own size. It was enough to make you want to join 4-H.

The only way to make out with a first-class girl, it seemed, was to be a fraternity man or a varsity athlete. It was almost impossible if you were a so-called "independent" and lived behind a furnace in a basement. I could always identify the athletes: They sneered a lot and they walked with a kind of lubricated swagger. Fraternity boys were easy to spot, too. They wore sport jackets to class and were always shouting hello to friends in an ostentatious manner and chuckling with them over parties they had been to. It made me sick.

My major didn't help any. Sanitary engineering was not

one of the glamour subjects. After six months as a student I hadn't had a single date. I didn't know one girl who wasn't going steady. Aside from Denise, no girl had taken even a momentary interest in me. Denise was a pro, but at least she wasn't pinned.

It was unfair. I had a lot to offer. I was good at math. I was pursuing a course of technical studies that would lead to a steady job at a fine salary. I was well along the road toward possessing an overwhelming vocabulary, though most of the words I was learning were hard to work into a conversation. I had a sweet nature and enjoyed a good joke as much as the next person. My face had good bone structure and a rapidly dwindling number of pustules. The rest of my body suffered from a ghastly paleness and tended toward the spindly, but there was no reason I would ever have to unveil it in direct light.

In comparison with my contemporaries, I suspected that the size and quality of my sexual organ fell somewhere in the middle range. While grossly underutilized, it showed no signs of atrophy, and I was confident that with reasonable care it would give me and my mate, if I ever found one, years of dependable service.

When I saw an attractive, unattached female at a sporting event, a lecture, or a campustown restaurant, which was seldom, I would try to work up enough nerve to speak to her. When I thought of a good opening gambit I worried about what I would say next if it was rebuffed. Trying to work out all the possibilities in advance meant that the initial overture was never made.

I spent weeks working on a printed statement that I could hand out on the street:

> My name is Thomas Shannon, San. Engr., Jr. If you are as intelligent and personable as you are good looking, we might be able to enter into a relationship we would both enjoy. May I buy you a Coke some afternoon? I'll say good-bye after thirty minutes whatever happens, so that's all the time I'm asking you to risk. If we hit it off I'll phone you later to ask for a date. At that time you can either accept or make an excuse. Use the attached postcard to give me your name and phone number.

113

It took many drafts to get the message this smooth and to give it what I thought was the proper tone. Nevertheless, it lacked something. If the girl didn't like my smile or the fleeting look she got at me, there wouldn't be enough reason for her to follow up. An intriguing paragraph about myself was needed. Despite hundreds of attempts, I couldn't find the right words. Short statements distorted me, long ones made me sound like a conceited windbag.

A direct approach might be better:

My name is Thomas Shannon. I'm a virgin and damned tired of it. Would you be so kind as to lend me your body some night soon? I will be extremely careful with it and will return it to you unharmed. The attached postcard is for your convenience. No stamp is necessary.

I didn't seriously consider that kind of note, of course. I wasn't about to give my cherry to just *anybody*. I had to find out first if she had any brains. I intended to lose my virginity to a *smart* woman and I wanted to *marry* a smart woman. You can't screw continuously even when your flesh is as flaming as mine was. A lot of the time you have to lie around and talk. I didn't want to find myself trapped in a bed with somebody who couldn't carry on an intelligent conversation. I wanted a sex partner just as smart as I was or even smarter, somebody who could help me make tough decisions, who was as interested as I was in the big questions of religion and science and sports, and who would join me in forging an ever-more-powerful vocabulary. A woman's brain was for me a kind of erogenous zone; a good one raised images in my mind of a rich, full life out of bed as well as in. A smart woman would reflect credit on me. I wanted to plunge my thing into somebody I was *proud* of.

And then, just when my cherry seemed most secure, when it seemed to be a nut that was not only uncrackable but unnoticed, it was suddenly in jeopardy. All because of a piece of paper that fluttered out of a library book.

17

What Tom Paine Said

The time had come to cram for the final in The Chemistry of Activated Sludge. I sat at my desk, clicked on my gooseneck, and opened Thomas Paine's *Age of Reason,* not a very intelligent thing to do academically. Here I had a hero of the American Revolution, an honest-to-God founding father, a man who some thought helped Thomas Jefferson write the Declaration of Independence, tearing the Bible and Christianity to shreds! And under what circumstances! He had gone to France in an effort to bring the blessing of revolution to that country and was locked up for his trouble. Expecting the guillotine momentarily, he set down his secret thoughts on religion. What he wrote hit me with the force of the Burlington Zephyr. Wielding logic, courage, and eloquence the way my mother did mops, Windex, and Sani-Flush, Paine swept out my mind, dusted my furniture, emptied my trashcans, threw open my shutters, and unclogged my drains. I couldn't stop reading. Some paragraphs made me want to jump to my feet and cheer! Finally questions were being satisfactorily answered!

According to Paine, Christianity is largely the concoction of what he calls Christian Mythologists:

> They represent this virtuous and amiable man, Jesus Christ, to be at once both God and Man, and also the Son of God, celestially begotten, on purpose to be sacri-

ficed, because they say that Eve in her longing had eaten an apple.

Putting aside everything that might excite laughter by its absurdity or detestation by its profaneness, it is impossible to conceive a story more derogatory to the Almighty, more inconsistent with his wisdom, more contradictory to his power, than this story is.

Oh, man, this was great stuff! I read it aloud to my roommates and they agreed. I turned hungrily to the section on the Bible. . . .

There are matters in that book, said to be done by the express command of God, that are as shocking to humanity and to every idea we have of moral justice as anything done by any assassin in modern times. When we read that the Israelites came by stealth upon whole nations of people, who, as history itself shows, had given them no offense; that they put all those nations to the sword; that they spared neither age nor infancy; that they left not a soul to breathe—are we sure these things are facts? Are we sure that the Creator commissioned these things to be done? Are we sure that the books that tell us so were written by his authority?

To believe the Bible to be true we must *unbelieve* all our belief in the moral justice of God. To read the Bible without horror, we must undo everything that is tender, sympathizing, and benevolent in the heart of man. Speaking for myself, if I had no other evidence that the Bible is fabulous than the sacrifice I must make to believe it to be true, that alone would be sufficient to determine my choice.

Speaking for me, too, Tom! I tried to read that passage aloud also, but Alex, Wayne, and Archy jumped on me, told me to pipe down, knock it off, and shut up, that they had studying to do. So I had to keep to myself the treasures that were spilling from this great book.

Revelation, when applied to religion, means something communicated *immediately* from God to man. No one will deny or dispute the power of the Almighty to make such a communication if he pleases. But admitting, for the sake of a case, that something has been revealed to

116

another person, it is revelation to that person only. When he tells it to a second person, a second to a third, a third to a fourth, and so on, it ceases to be a revelation to all those persons. It is revelation to the first person only, and *hearsay* to every other, and consequently they are not obliged to believe it.

When I am told that a woman called the Virgin Mary said that she was with child without any cohabitation with a man, and that her husband, Joseph, said that an angel told him so, I have a right to believe them or not; such a circumstance requires a much stronger evidence than their bare word for it; but we have not even this—for neither Joseph nor Mary wrote any such matter themselves; it is hearsay upon hearsay, and I do not choose to rest upon such evidence.

Neither do I, Tom! I turned a page. A piece of orange paper floated to my lap. On it was a mimeographed message:

If you checked out this book you should check out our organization—
    THE IOWA STATE FREE THOUGHT CLUB
—Dedicated to the untrammeled freedom of the human mind, to the inalienable right to follow truth wherever it may lead, and to the effort to loosen the grip of organized religion's dead hand wherever it has fastened itself on to the soaring flights of the human spirit and civilized progress.
    Do you doubt some of the things you were taught at your mother's knee? You are not alone. Meet with us Wednesday nights at 8:00 in the recreation room of the Unitarian Church. Coffee. Doughnuts. Bring a friend.

It was Wednesday. I decided to go. There would be time to bone up on activated sludge when the meeting was over.

So consumed was I at that moment by the novelty and rightness of my new convictions that I made a foolish mistake. I put my trust in a blood relative and was honest with her. It was stupid of me because her freedom was still very much trammeled. She was my first cousin Carolyn. She had married a Fleckenstein and was living in Hazel Green, Wisconsin, where she and her husband were in the cheese game. A letter from her had arrived several days before and was lying unanswered on my desk.

Hi Tommy!

My baby finally arrived and I got your address from your mother. Frank and I want you to be the Godfather. You are still a Catholic in good standing, aren't you? (Ha ha) When are you coming home next? We can plan the Baptism then. Our place or your place. (Ha ha)
Write sometime!

> Your cousin,
> Carolyn
> (and Frank says hello)

I dashed off a reply I was later to regret.

Dear Carolyn,

It was an honor to be asked to serve as Godfather, but if you feel I have to be a Catholic, then I must refuse. I left the Church quite some time ago.
Don't bother arguing with me because my decision is immutable. And don't tell my mother and father, as it would get them all upset over a fait accompli that is over and done with.
Remember: not a word to anyone!

> Still your cousin,
> Tommy

18

Atheist Poetry

The meeting of the Iowa State Free Thought Club came to order with only six men and three women in attendance. The other seventeen members, it was guessed, were studying for finals. Those present voted 8–0 with one abstention (mine) to delay the scheduled election of officers for two weeks. President Hugh Findley sent a note apologizing for his absence and expressing the hope that the elections would be held so that the workload could be shifted to other shoulders. He said he was well pleased with the progress that had been made during his term in office, progress that would have been impossible without the support and hard work of all the members, for which he was deeply thankful, singling out especially Barry, Rachel, Dick, and Stu.

With Treasurer Dick Pittinger not present, Vice President Barry Cox asked Rachel Isaacs to give a review of "the financial end of things." Rachel Isaacs turned out to be the studious-looking girl sitting next to me who smelled of jasmine. She rose and explained that dues for the coming quarter were now payable and the sooner the better. The bank balance stood at $2.37, as compared with a standing debt of $4.35 for mimeo paper. She was the slim, trim type, probably better than me at tennis. Her face was striking rather than beautiful, with a straight, thin nose, eyes that were enlarged by her glasses, very black eyebrows

119

and hair, and skin that was accented by freckles. By the vocabulary she used in addressing the group it was plain that she was much above average in intelligence, and so I wondered what it would be like to talk to her, hold her hand, kiss her, marry her, and sexually congress her. When she sat down she looked at me and blushed a little, smiling in a way that made me almost certain that I was in love with her.

"Your first time here?" she asked softly.

I nodded, blushing in return. She made a quieting gesture with her hand that I took to mean "Relax—everything is going to be okay."

Stu Perkins wasn't there, so somebody named Jim gave a report on the activities of the Accreditation Committee. From his remarks I was able to gather that the club was not recognized as a legitimate student organization and therefore was not permitted to advertise in the college newspaper, post notices on campus bulletin boards, or hold meetings on school property. Jim said that Dr. Bennington, Dean of Student Affairs, was sympathetic but assured him that the student-faculty senate had considered the application for the last time this school year. The only chance now was the election of a more liberal slate of students in the next fall quarter.

Somebody suggested suing the school on constitutional grounds, but that was thrown out for lack of funds.

Rachel said she thought the club should defy the ban against use of campus bulletin boards as a means of publicizing the school's prejudice, which set off a lively debate. It was decided by a narrow vote that nothing even faintly illegal or aggressive should be undertaken lest the forces ranged against reason be given a way to portray the members as a pack of lawbreakers and fanatics, a decision that made Rachel shake her head and purse her lips in frustration. She was well bred and probably came from a good home.

A blond girl announced that she had finally found the Washington, D.C., address of Paul Blanshard and had written to extend to him the hospitality and the platform of the club next time he was in the Ames area.

A young man reported that he had not yet had any success in getting in to see anybody important on his proposal for eliminating the benediction from the graduation ceremony.

"What's your name?" Rachel asked suddenly. When I told her, she stood up and addressed the group. "We have a visitor with us tonight," she said, ignoring my gestures of alarm. "He's going to tell us about himself and how he happens to be here." She tugged at my sleeve and smiled encouragingly.

Amid light clapping I struggled to my feet. That was a mistake. They couldn't have found a worse public speaker if they had conducted a nationwide talent hunt. My cheeks and ears grew hot, and the hand of panic tightened around my throat; why, I don't know, because everybody looked interested and friendly enough. "Well, I was reading *Age of Reason*," I said in a voice I didn't recognize as mine, "and I saw your leaflet, which is how—or was how—I learned out about the club. *Learned* about it. Found out about it." A profound feeling of certainty came over me that I was an idiot, and I glanced down at Rachel to see if she was feeling the same thing. That was another mistake, because the expression on her face was almost painfully endearing. "That's a great book," I said, looking away from her. "A really great book." For safety I fixed my gaze on a wall. "A terrific book. The leaflet was not too bad, either." My mind was very nearly a blank, and I couldn't think of any of the concrete words of color and punch that Wilfred Funk had been urging on me for years. With a minute to think and calm down I could have called the book "seminal" and "fecund," "grandiloquent," even. "I wanna join up, that's for sure. Did I say my name was Thomas Shannon? Tom? I'm all for the untrammeled freedom of the human mind. Sold on it." My knees were quivering inside my pantlegs and my heart was pounding so hard I was afraid the vibrations could be seen on my shirt. "I'm from Dubuque. Where Iowa, Wisconsin, and Illinois come together. I can see them all from my bedroom. My bedroom there, not my bedroom here. There is nothing like *Age of Reason* or this club in Dubuque, I can tell you that. This club is great." It was desperately important that I make a good impression on these people. I was burning my bridges behind me, tearing away from the grasp of my family and shoving off toward unknown shores in a boat full of strangers. If my new shipmates didn't approve of me or thought I was stupid, the rest of my life was going to be a nightmare. More precisely, it was Rachel's esteem that was vital. If she accepted me I could happily jettison the rest. To impress her and show everybody I was far from stupid, I tried to think of some good words to use. Once they got an inkling of the breadth and depth of my vocabulary there would be no question of my acceptability and I would have made a whole group of new friends. But for some reason the only ones I could come up with were *contrapuntal* and *plangent*. I hesitated as long as I dared, searching for a way to work them in, then gave up and told them I was an engineering student. That was smart on my part, because engineering students weren't expected to be able to speak at all, much less use evocative and muscular words. "I just recently got out of looking at everything from the religious point of view," I said, now glancing from face to face. "Finding you people is really great and means a lot to me. I have enough money for the dues, so that's no problem." One of the difficulties I was having was that my voice refused to stay in a register that anybody was familiar with. "I hope you'll take me as a member, because I—" I don't remember how I was planning to end that sentence. I sat down abruptly when I got the distinct impression that I was going to cry. I do remember a warm round of applause. Apparently the flood of sincerity at the end made up for the various flaws in my presentation.

Rachel leaned toward me and whispered, "What religion were you raised in?" When I told her she touched my arm and said, "I'm so sorry."

After a few book reports from several members—which included a rave for one I had checked out but had not yet read: *Man and His Gods* by Homer W. Smith—Vice President Cox moved into the highlight of the evening, a recitation of poems by somebody named G. L. Mackenzie, as selected and arranged by Charles Smith, President of the American Society for the Advancement of Atheism.

The poetry was excellent. Rachel and I, exchanging blushes and smiles, enjoyed it tremendously.

The New Doxology
by G. L. Mackenzie

Praise God from whom all cyclones blow
Praise him when rivers overflow,
Praise him who whirls down house and steeple
Who sinks the ship and drowns the people.
For parsons who with hood and bell
Demand your cash or threaten hell,
Praise God for war, for strife and pain,
For earthquake shocks; and then,
Let all men cry aloud, Amen.

Where Was God?
When early man, impelled by fate,
Pursued his kind with savage hate,
Made slaves of some, and others ate,
　　　Where were thou, O God?
When devastating robber bands
Invaded peaceful, fruitful lands,
And steeped in blood their ruthless hands,
　　　Where wert thou, O God?
When priests and kings and other knaves
Made human minds and bodies slaves
And gloated o'er their victims' graves,
　　　Where wert thou, O God?

This was strong stuff, and I was tingling from head to foot. I was excited by the poetry, I was excited by Rachel, and I was excited by the mere fact of *being* there. These people were relaxed, friendly, fabulously sophisticated, and they were atheists! It was fantastic.

Belated Atonement
A third part of Jehovah died
　　To stop the other two
From having men forever fried
　　And roasted through and through.
Now God, look here! I've read your book,
　　And if I'm not a fool,
It clearly shows your anger took
　　Four thousand years to cool!
For if you'd wished to purify
　　And save men's souls from hell,
Why was it that you didn't die
　　The day that Adam fell?

Away with Priests

Away with parsons and with priests!
    But why?
Because they falsely claim to know
That God exists, and strive to show
That they're his agents here below,
    That's why!
Away with parsons and with priests!
    But why?
Because they hold a bunch of tracts
That tell of ancient, monstrous acts
Of gods and beasts and say they're facts,
    That's why!
Away with parsons and with priests!
    But why?
Because they've filled the earth with fears,
Dissension, hopeless hopes and tears,
Throughout a thousand wasted years,
    That's why!

Vice President Cox wished everybody good luck on their exams, then, neatly continuing the theme of the evening, closed the meeting by asking everyone to join him in reciting Swinburne's immortal words in praise of the finality of death:

From too much love of living,
    From hope and fear set free,
We thank with brief thanksgiving
    Whatever gods may be
That no life lives forever;
    That dead men rise up never;
That even the weariest river
    Winds somewhere safe to sea.

Then stars nor sun shall waken,
    Nor any change of light;
Nor sound of waters shaken
    Nor any sound or sight;
Nor wintry leaves nor vernal,
    Nor days nor things diurnal;
Only the sleep eternal
    In an eternal night.

It was my lucky day! Rachel was as interested in me as I was in her, and we shared the most delicious coffee and doughnut it has ever been my privilege to enjoy. She told me that it was an act of true bravery on my part to break out of the Catholic religion, which built a heavier wall around its members than any other. I said, Oh, hell, it wasn't as hard as all that. She said I showed a great deal of strength, that she had been deeply moved by my statement to the club, and that she could well imagine—and here she touched my arm again—the turmoil in my heart.

I walked her home. I didn't have to ask her . . . it was inevitable and didn't have to be articulated. We left the building together and struck out for her place as if it were the most natural thing in the world. We conversed quickly, trying to learn as much about each other as we could in the shortest possible time. I had never met anyone I could talk to so easily; there was no sense of awkwardness.

By the time we had gone six blocks she was the best friend I had in the world, knew more about me, and understood me better.

I told her about my family, she told me about hers. She had to tell me she was Jewish, something she was amazed I hadn't deduced from her name. I said she didn't look Jewish and that one of my best friends—I was thinking of Alex—was Jewish. She laughed gaily, thinking I had made a deliberate joke. Mystified, I pretended that I had.

She was from Kansas City. Her father was some sort of corrugated cardboard-box tycoon, her mother a warrior for Jewish charities. Despite their concern for financial security and their acceptance of Judaism, along with other shortcomings she didn't specify, she loved them. I told her my parents weren't perfect, either, but I loved them just the same. That put us in a difficult position, she said. It was much harder to reject the religion of your parents if you loved them. If you hated them, then it was easy. I told her that was the profoundest thing I had ever heard. I had read a number of profound things, of course, but what she had just said was the most profound thing I had ever heard anybody actually *say*.

She lived at Omicron Epsilon Mu, a house I had always heard referred to as Omicron Epsilon, Nu? It was the only Jewish sorority in the state. We stood halfway up the marble steps and talked. Six or eight other couples stood motionlessly and kissed at various points on the steps and lawn. We pretended not to see them. I looked at her in the soft glow of the porch light. Earlier I thought she was merely striking-looking, now I could see that she was extraordinarily beautiful. It was amazing how different two Jews could be: Rachel was a goddess, Alex Gold was a beast. She smelled of flowers, he of sweat. She was sleek, he was scaly. It taught me an important lesson. It was not always a good idea to assume that one person is typical of a whole race or nation. I should have known that already. I was Irish, yet highballs turned my stomach.

She was majoring in business administration, she was telling me, and minoring in art.

"My father thinks it's the other way around. He wanted me to have only a touch of business courses so that my husband wouldn't be able to put anything over on me, but to get a degree in art, which would be more appropriate for a woman. He's going to die when I graduate from the business school instead of the art school."

"I'll bet!"

"As long as I'm spending all this time at college, I figure I might as well get a degree that's worth something. I don't want to spend my best years in a kitchen, talking to babies. I intend to get a job when I get out, and so I want to be qualified for a *good* job. Can you blame me for not wanting to be somebody's flunky?"

"Absolutely not!"

"Not that art isn't important to me. It's very important. I think art and beauty and truth are the most important things in life, don't you?"

"You're darned right I do! I'm in the arts myself, so to speak."

"Oh? Fine or performing?"

"Technological. The technological arts. Sanitary engineering."

"I thought that had to do with . . ."

"It does, but I look at it a little differently. Beauty and art are to some extent the absence of ugliness. Now you take a landscape. On the right is a stagnant pond covered with scum. On the left is an open dump. In the center is a woods ruined by stumps and snags. *Uproot* the stumps, cut *down* the snags, cover the dump with a clean, inorganic fill, aerate the pond and bring its pH down to 7.4 or 7.3, and what have you got? You've got a landscape worth looking at. You've got beauty. You've got art."

She looked at me admiringly.

"Without modern systems of sanitation and waste disposal," I raved, "civilization itself wouldn't be possible. Garbage, sewage, and filth would be piled up higher than our heads—nothing could live in a mess like that, certainly not an *artist*. What sanitary engineers do is provide an environment—an ambience, if you will—in which art and artists can function and burgeon. Not only that, there is good money in it. Say I had a wife in the business world who wanted to quit for a while to paint and have a baby. I want to have a salary that would give her the freedom to do that if she wanted to."

The porch light began blinking. There was ten-thirty curfew for undergraduate women on weeknights.

"Oh-oh," Rachel said, "that's the signal. I have to go in. I enjoyed the evening . . . I can't *tell* you."

"I'll call you sometime," I said suavely.

I could have kissed her, but I didn't try. I said good night and left, proving to her that I liked her for herself and not for her body. I skipped happily home knowing that my life had changed forever.

19

Certain Important Matters

Dear Tommy,

I thought your father was getting better and then Carolyn sent me your letter and now I don't know. The Doctor was here today. You have turned your back on God? I can't believe you would do it, make such a terrible mistake, a boy like you who talks so well and with your brain. Oh, if you only knew how many hearts you have broken with that ugly letter . . . we are all just *sick* about it. I don't know if you can even read my writing my hand is shaking so.

I know it is wonderful to be young and in college and think you know all the answers, but you should get down on your knees and ask God to forgive you. Your Catholic faith is the greatest thing you'll ever have . . . *don't lose it.*

I knew I shouldn't have let you go back when you were here, you were sick and weak and not yourself. You would never do a thing like this and you are going through a phase.

If you could make me understand why. Why? How could you do it? At least carry your Badge of the Sacred Heart in your wallet.

Your mother and father

Dear Mom and Dad,

Tell Carolyn to stay out of my way because if I see her I'm liable to let her have it. I told her a secret and she blabbed first chance she got. Why she wanted to cause you and Dad this grief I don't know; I would never have told you because I don't think I can make you understand. I will try when I see you if you want to talk about it. For now I will only say that I can't believe in God after what happened in Portugal in 1755 and Italy in 1769.

On All Souls' Day in Lisbon in 1755 people were packed into churches and an earthquake struck and killed thousands of them. To get away from falling churches, people ran out on a pier and got killed by a tidal wave. Something like sixty thousand died! Those poor Portuguese weren't drinking and gambling, Mom, they were praying on All Souls' Day!

And then, in San Nazaro, Italy, there was a church basement where the Republic of Venice stored gunpowder. In 1769 the lightning rod had been around for seventeen years, but the priest and the parishioners would have nothing to do with such a scientific gadget, counting on processions and ringing the steeple bell to protect them. A storm came up and you can guess what happened. Lightning struck, the powder exploded, and thousands more innocent people were killed. I'm sorry, but I'm not going to try anymore to believe in a God who would let things like that happen.

And I'm not going to carry the Badge of the Sacred Heart in my wallet. Have you ever looked at it? It shows a human heart dripping blood, on fire, wrapped in thorns. It's gory! I've been doing some reading lately and I know now that it is a superstition based on ignorance of what the heart is for, a carryover from pagans who worshipped all sorts of organs. The Church should have abandoned it in 1614 when William Harvey discovered that the heart was a pump.

I'm telling you this so you will see that it is useless to argue with me because the facts are all on my side. When I come home next I might be able to get you to see it my way.

You will be happy to hear that since leaving the Church I haven't had any trouble with asthma. Not one wheeze. Don't tell me that's a coincidence.

I met a wonderful girl you would like. She's Jewish and I'll probably marry her eventually.

How is Dad doing? Back on his feet yet?

With Love,
Tommy

Alex, Wayne, and Archy called a special meeting to discuss "certain important matters." They made me sit with them at the kitchen table. They were oddly serious and ill at ease, especially Archy and Alex, who acted as if they would rather be dead, or at least elsewhere. Wayne's natural aura of gloom was well suited to the carrying out of distasteful chores.

"What's up?" I asked. Except for the hum of the furnace fan, the room was strangely quiet.

Wayne acted as spokesman for the three of them. "Shannon, we are your best friends. We give you a hard time now and then, but we're the best you've got. As far as we know, you don't even have any other friends."

I didn't like the sound of this.

"We've been watching you lately and we're getting a little worried. You've been acting like . . . a rudderless ship."

"More like a chicken with its head cut off," said Archy.

I laughed nervously. "Aw, you guys are just jealous because I've got such a terrific girl friend," I felt my ears turn red.

"We'll get to her in a minute. Now, we can't tell you what to do, but we've talked things over and decided that we should at least ask you to consider a few points. After all, Alex and Archy and I are responsible for you."

"Wait just a minute! How do you figure you are responsible for me?"

"We took you in. We gave you shelter. We accepted you into our little family here, such as it is. You were like a shell-shocked refugee washed up on a beach. We molded you."

"You didn't *mold* me. . . . I know what I'm doing!"

"Let me finish. Maybe we didn't mold you, exactly. We *influenced* you."

Alex, slumped in his chair, snorted. "I think we *molded* the little putz."

"You've got to admit," Archy said, "you were sort of a creep when you moved in. You hardly said a word for days. All we heard from you were wheezes." His beady eyes had been darting nervously here and there; now they were on me.

"Then when you did start talking we couldn't shut you up," Alex said. "All that religious stuff. God this and God that, sin this and sin that. You nearly drove us nuts."

"Yeah, but you were heckling me. I had to defend myself."

"We know that," Wayne said. "We feel now that we ganged up on you, came down on you too hard. We weren't, ah, sensitive to the tension, we didn't realize that you were sorting yourself out and that the, well, ridicule we subjected you to might be picking up more weight than might have been the case ordinarily."

"You were fouled up and we were making it worse," Alex said.

"The whorehouse trip was our idea," Wayne said. "We forced it on you."

"Are you kidding? I didn't have to go if I didn't want to."

"No, we put the pressure on. You would have looked chicken if you had backed out. So we feel responsible for what happened on the trip."

"What do you mean, 'what happened'? *Nothing* happened!"

"That's a laugh," said Alex. "All the way to Springfield you were in the pulpit. In the whorehouse you called down the wrath of God on our heads and damned us all to hell. Then you ditched us. We thought you were going off to become a nun. When you got back to Ames you told us that the Church is full of crap, God is a fake, and the Pope is queer."

"You guys flatter yourselves," I said. "That was building up for years. I would have reached the same conclusions if I had never met you, even if I had stayed at Catholic House."

"Maybe so," said Wayne, "but not so suddenly. Not so recklessly. If we had been more aware of your problems—more sympathetic—you might not have . . . what shall I say . . . lost your bearings."

131

"Suppose you tell me how I have lost my bearings. I have been under perfect control at all times." I started to get up. Wayne waved me down.

"Do us the favor of hearing us out. This isn't easy for us. By losing your bearings I meant that you wasted two whole quarters. You didn't cram for your exams. You cut classes. First you spent all your time rehashing religious wars that nobody has worried about for hundreds of years. Soon as you got over that, you went crazy over a girl. Shannon, we want to know something. Did you flunk all your courses?"

They had me. In the scholastic sense I had lost my bearings. Right when I had to hit my sewage books the hardest I didn't open them at all. I hit books, but not books having anything to do with my exams. I didn't do what had to be done. I lost track of why I was at school. I don't know why. I knew I was digging my own grave, but for some reason I wouldn't let myself think about it.

"You did flunk, didn't you?" Wayne asked this in a very soft voice, as if trying to minimize the pain. I knew he was smart; what I didn't know is that he had feelings.

I stared at the floor. "I got my grades yesterday," I said faintly. "Two C's, two D's, and an F."

"You know what that means, don't you? Getting below a C average two quarters in a row?"

"It means I've flunked out. It means I've got to sit out a quarter. It means I might get drafted." I put my hand over my eyes. How would I ever tell Rachel and my parents? They thought I was so smart.

"We thought so," said Wayne. "Now, listen. You have one last chance. You told us your faculty adviser was Old Main Kellman and that you hit it off pretty well with him. Isn't that right?"

I nodded. I couldn't speak. A lump had formed in my throat at the thought of these three guys, all older than me, trying to help and trying to be sincere. It was even more agonizing for them than it was for me.

"They'll let you register for the third quarter if you appeal for a review of your case by the Eligibility Committee of the student-faculty senate. Ask Doc Kellman to demand that you be given probationary status. He can say you had asthma and that now you're over it."

"Would that work?" I was almost afraid to let myself have any hope.

"It might. The administration is scared to death of Kellman. He can get them denounced in the papers any time he wants to just by saying he's being harassed. It's amazing how many people there are who don't want Old Main torn down."

"I'll go see him right away."

"Wait, there's more. If it works and they let you stay, you've got to buckle down. You've got to *study*, Shannon. You've got to study *sewage*."

"I'll do it!" I said, banging my fist on the table. "I know I'm smarter than most of the other guys in the class. Can I go now? Are you through? I appreciate the advice—no kidding, I mean it—but I've got an appointment." I had no appointment. I just wanted to get out of there for everybody's sake. I wanted to go to the student union and play Ping-Pong with somebody I didn't know and would never see again.

"One more thing," Wayne said. "Our final point. You won't survive if you keep carrying on the way you have been with this girl friend of yours."

"What has she got to do with it?"

"Plenty. You've got to stop seeing so much of her. Confine her to weekends."

"To weekends! I don't think I could! I love her! I'm thinking of marrying her!"

"Come on, Shannon," Alex said in annoyance, breaking what for him was a long silence. "You don't have to marry her just because you want to play hide-the-wienie."

"You dirty . . ."

"Love her on weekends," Wayne said. "Study on weekdays. When you get your grades up, then do whatever you want."

"Give her up on weekdays. . . . Oh, God . . . she's everything I ever wanted. . . ."

"You're throwing yourself at her," Wayne said. "That's no good. Think. Nobody is as terrific as you say she is. Your emotions have taken you over. To get hold of yourself, think about her weak points."

"She doesn't have any."

They had me cornered again. Rachel was a human

being; she must have something wrong with her. I knew it wasn't rational to be blind to her shortcomings, to be so happy when I was with her. Maybe my roommates could help me clear my mind.

"Suppose we call your attention to a weak point or two," Wayne said. "I'll begin. She used you during finals, therefore she is selfish. You helped her study for *her* exams, she didn't help you with yours. Yours went out the window."

"I let her think I was so smart I didn't have to study."

"If she was concerned with anything but herself she wouldn't have believed you. So she is selfish. Or dumb. Take your pick. Archy?"

"She's not beautiful," Archy said. "Too thin. A nice-looking girl. Not beautiful."

"She *is* beautiful," I said.

"She isn't beautiful," Archy said.

"You wouldn't know beauty if you fell into a tub of it," I said.

"She's a nice-looking Jewish girl," Alex said with an air of finality, "not a beautiful Jewish girl. Listen, I've seen beautiful Jewish girls."

"Way too thin," Archy insisted. "Christ, you'd wake up in the morning covered with puncture wounds."

I didn't get mad. They were trying to help me by cutting Rachel down to human terms. I not only had her on a pedestal, I had her floating above it.

"Well, she's beautiful to me," I said.

"That's better," Wayne said.

The three of them exchanged glances that indicated they felt progress was being made.

"Looks aren't all that important, anyway," I said.

"We didn't say they were. We are merely trying to make you see that you've been exaggerating things to yourself. Remember that you met her on the rebound. You went from the arms of the Church to the arms of the first halfway-acceptable girl that smiled at you. Keep that in mind. Alex?"

"She lives at Omicron Ep. A whole houseful of rich Jewish snots. I tell you, Shannon, they are nothing but trouble. Get a lower-class Jewish girl and you'll have something. This girl of yours, her father is some kind of Kansas City box king. When he hears his daughter is running around with a goy who lives behind a furnace, the son of an Irish-Catholic barber, what do you think will happen? His yarmulke will go right through the ceiling! I know these rich Jews! They stick together! If she balks they'll yank her out of school so fast you'll think she's tied to a rubber band."

That was too much. Now I did get mad. "Alex, you are so full of crap I don't see how you keep it from leaking out. That you and Rachel Isaacs can both be called Jews makes the term practically meaningless. Let me tell *you* something for a change. If the ancient Hebrews had had more people like Rachel and fewer like you, they never would have been run out of Egypt."

Alex looked at Wayne and Archy and shrugged. "At least," he said, "the broad is teaching him some history."

They laughed at that remark. I didn't. I sat staring at the table. They stood up and moved to their desks, where they snapped on lamps and opened textbooks. Wayne leaned back in his chair and slapped me on the shoulder to buck me up.

There were long minutes of silence. Directly overhead I heard the muffled sound of someone changing position. I suppose Mrs. Parkhurst had her ear to the furnace grating and now had a crick in her neck.

Finally I got to my feet and put on my coat. After standing by the door for a while I managed to mutter a thank you. Nobody looked up. They grunted their responses and shifted their feet.

Outside I was greeted by a cold wind. I walked to the remotest corner of the campus, beyond the hog barns, and sat on a tree stump. I stayed there for an hour thinking about what a mess I had made of things and how amazing it was that my hard-boiled roommates thought enough of me to meddle in my life.

20

The Persuasion of Rachel

The glow from the streetlight was cut off by the giant hydrangeas that lined the front of the Omicron Epsilon Mu sorority house. There was no moon. Behind the bushes I was in the arms of the first halfway-acceptable girl who had smiled at me, and she was in mine. We kissed hungrily, leaning against the building to keep our balance. Our lips yielded and the tips of our tongues touched, tentatively at first, then more boldly, advancing and retreating by turns. In a burst of passion we mashed our lips and teeth together, letting our tongues slip and slide past each other like lunging fish. Two feet to the south my organ of sexual reproduction threw off its chains and rose brazenly outward and upward, carrying my shorts and pants along with it, creasing Rachel's skirt and coming to rest somewhere on her lower abdominal area. My right hand went completely berserk, burrowing through sweaters and blouses and slips until it found the cup of a brassiere.

The porch light began blinking.

I drew back, startled. I thought for a moment that I had driven Rachel against the sorority house with such force that I had tripped some sort of gigantic "Tilt!" mechanism.

"Damn!" I said.

"Whew!" she said, laughing and straightening her clothes. "Saved by the bell!"

* * *

The next day I was waiting for her when she got out of her first class. I took her to Lake LaVerne and the bench on which I had skipped Mass a lifetime ago.

"Rachel," I said, "I can't stand it anymore. Getting worked up over and over without any release is ruining my health. I can't study. My grades are suffering. We've got to quit carrying on like a couple of sophomores."

"I *am* a sophomore."

"That doesn't make any difference. The frustration is just too much. Holding myself back . . . it's murder."

"I know what you mean. I don't like it, either."

"Look, we are two mature people. Think how lucky we are, not being bound and gagged by religious restrictions. We don't have to punish ourselves like this."

She looked at the lake, then said, "I want to make you happy, not miserable. Maybe we shouldn't fool around so much. A hands-off policy."

"That would be a hundred times worse. When I'm with you I want to touch you, when I touch you I want to kiss you, when . . . Rachel, do you love me?"

"I . . . I think so. I'm sure I do."

"Well, I think so and I'm sure I do, too. So let's do what lovers are supposed to do. Let's quit the high-school stuff."

"Are you thinking of actual sexual intercourse?"

"Yes."

"Oh, God, going all the way is so . . . so *symbolic.*"

"Of course it's symbolic! Why can't we be symbolic if we want to?"

"It's dangerous. It stirs up such deep emotions. . . ."

I had a vision of a steel poker plunged into red-hot coals, stirring up unimaginably deep emotions.

"We say we love each other, but we aren't sure," I said. "By stirring up a few emotions we might find out one way or the other. At least we would prove that we are serious. We should give ourselves to each other without let or hindrance."

"Do we have to talk about it in the glare of the sun? About one of the most important things in life?"

"Would you rather talk about it behind the hydrangea bushes? When we are so hot we can't think straight?"

She sighed and fiddled with a twig. "Maybe going to bed

with you would prove that I'm finally making my own decisions about things that count."

"I couldn't have put it better myself!"

"But it might be the wrong decision."

"Rachel, we've got to do it. For our self-respect. And for my peace of mind. I can't study because I think about making love to you all the time. If we could go all the way once in a while, say on weekends, I could turn my mind to my studies on weekdays."

"Sleeping together might make it worse."

"It couldn't be worse. I'm like a bomb about to go off. How do you think it makes me feel, being an atheist and a virgin? It makes me feel like an idiot. Now I meet a girl I love who's an atheist, too, and she is afraid. She doesn't want to. If you love me I don't see why you don't want to."

"I didn't say I didn't want to. Only that I wasn't sure it would lead us in the right direction. It would change our relationship."

"For the better."

"Maybe. There is something you should know. I might as well tell you now as later. As my mother would say, I can't give you the gift of my virginity."

"So take the gift of *my* virginity! Take it! I want you to have it! I don't want it! I don't care about yours. Yours doesn't mean anything to me at all."

"I'm glad it's not important. But I had to tell you."

"Anybody I know?"

"No."

"Somebody from the club? President Findley? Vice President Cox?"

"No. I thought you didn't care."

"I don't. Just curious. Just wondering who the lucky guy was."

"It was a boy I talked my parents into taking along on vacation a couple of summers ago. He said he couldn't stand holding back, just like you. If we didn't shtup, he said, he'd lose his mind. I gave in. We shtupped. Then that's all he wanted to do, day and night, shtup, shtup, shtup. It didn't calm him down at all. It steamed him up all the more."

"So you quit?"

"When we got back to Kansas City I never wanted to see him again. We had nothing in common intellectually. It was fun, sort of, but when it was over I felt used."

"It's different with us. We have a lot in common intellectually. And what's more, we're both cool and logical and objective."

"That's true."

"I mean more to you than that guy did, don't I?"

"Yes."

"So give me what you gave him."

"It's not the same. I shouldn't have given him anything. He was only interested in my body."

"Not me. I love your brain, too. I loved your brain first. Now I want to love your body. Is there anything wrong with that?"

"No."

"Feeling the way we do about each other, given the torture I am going through, for us not to sleep together would only mean one thing. That our parents and our former religions are running us by remote control. Isn't that right?"

"I guess so. I don't know."

"Can you give me one single reason based on scientific fact why we shouldn't go to bed together? One reason that doesn't come from the goddam Judeo-Christian ethic?"

"No."

"There isn't a one, is there?"

"No."

"So your answer is yes?"

"No. I mean, wait. Let me think. I don't want to rush into this." I started to kiss her. "Don't touch me. I can't think when you are touching me. Give me a minute." She turned away. "I am fully capable of making up my own mind."

I looked at the sheen of her black hair, the ribbon on her ponytail. I resisted the impulse to trace the curve of her waist and hips. I wanted to slip my hands under her arms and smother her breasts. I put my head on the back of the bench and closed my eyes, waiting for the jury to return with a verdict. The spring sun tried to warm my face.

There was a slight noise and movement. I smelled flowers and felt Rachel's breath. I opened my eyes and saw her face an inch from mine. She was smiling. She encircled me with her arms. She kissed my nose and lips.

"Okay," she said.

It was not to be an easy deflowering. Days were needed to work out a plan that suited her sense of propriety. She didn't want to take part in anything as deeply symbolic and potentially beautiful as the melding and merging of two human beings if it involved back seats of cars or hydrangea bushes. What finally evolved was this: An hour after "lights out" at her sorority she would slip down a back staircase that led to the basement. There, following an escape route blazed by countless Omicron Eps before her, a chain of nameless adventurers that stretched back into the swirling mists of time, she would climb atop crates of canned goods to a high window where she could, by pushing with her feet against a reinforced concrete structural haunch, propel herself into the night. A block away I would be waiting with four empty suitcases in a borrowed, rented, or stolen car that would take us to an obscure motel on the Des Moines River near Boone, twenty miles west, where we would register as Mr. and Mrs. Julian Huxley. An alarm clock going off at 4:38 A.M. would send us back along the road we came. Rachel would be in her proper bed before the first rays of the sun hit the top of the campanile.

I don't know what I would have done without my roommates, who put me in a debt I'll never be able to repay. Archy had never lent his car to anyone for any reason, but he insisted on lending it to me. He even threw in a tune-up and two gallons of gas. It was, as Alex stressed, "an unprecedented occasion: the deflowering of a lower-class Dubuque Irish ex-Catholic by a snotty Kansas City Jewish cardboard-box heiress. In a Boone motel! Do you realize what the odds are against such a thing ever happening? Save the registration receipt. I can sell photostats of it by mail."

They reviewed Rachel's alleged weak points again in an effort to shore up my aplomb. I was headed for a delicate rite of passage; they wanted me to conduct myself as a credit to my gender and not as a slobbering puppy. Alex pointed out that recent remarks of hers amounted to cultural aggression—Semitism, he called it. Great musicians, she had said, were the loftiest peaks of human evolution. Their performances represented the ultimate in intelligence, sensitivity, discipline, artistry, and coordination. I had to agree. The most difficult instrument of all to master, she said, was the violin. I said that was no doubt true. Days later she added a final thought: All great violinists are Jewish. I didn't even connect the two conversations; Alex did it for me when I reported them. He admired her insidiousness. She knew goddam well, he said, or she wouldn't have raised the subject, that there weren't any Irish violinists. I wasn't convinced by his argument, but I didn't argue. I was pretty sure that a bit of research in the library would uncover an Irish violinist.

Alex spent an hour washing the car, including the dents and scratches. He tried valiantly to polish the rusted hubcaps and the battered hood ornament, and when he was done he sprayed his work with perfume and consecrated it with a Hebrew prayer. Wayne borrowed an extension cord from Mrs. Parkhurst and vacuumed the interior until it smelled like a new rug. The old heap looked great.

Time to go. They shook hands with me in turn.

"I want to wish you the best of luck," Wayne said somberly, dropping into my shirt pocket a packet containing one of the very best reservoir-tipped prophylactics.

"Go get her, kid," said Alex, adding a slap on the back.

"Have a nice time," Archy said. "I only ask one thing. Don't get cock tracks on the upholstery."

21

A Problem in Smegma

I swung the car off the highway. The headlights swept the whitewashed walls of the Riverview Motel, "Boone's Finest."

"Stop the car," Rachel cried.

"What? Why?"

"Stop right here! Please!"

I stepped on the brake. The car skidded to a stop on the gravel driveway. "What's the matter?"

"I want to see what the place looks like. Is this it?"

"This is it."

"Are you sure?"

"I'm sure."

"We have to drive through that archway to get to our rooms?"

"To our room."

"Right past the clerk? Isn't there a back way?"

"This is the only entrance. We are not going to just drive through the archway, we are going to park under it while I go in and register."

"He'll see me!"

"So what? He doesn't give a shit. He's just in it for the money."

"He'll think I'm just in it for the money, too."

"Mrs. Julian Huxley? Please."

"They might not have any more rooms."

"That big neon sign that says Vacancy? It means they have a vacancy. Rachel, for the love of God, you aren't going to back out *now*. . . ."

"It's so sleazy," she said, grimacing. "It'll be filthy. There'll be cockroaches. Can't we find a cabin on a nice lake somewhere with some privacy? Something clean? With a little *charm*?"

"In the middle of the night? You didn't tell me it had to be like your folks's place in Florida."

"Look! He sees us! The clerk!"

"Of course he sees us! We're shining our headlights right in his face."

"Oh, Tommy, I'm sorry. I can't bring myself to go into a place like that . . . past that man. I'd feel like a *whore*. Can't we drive around awhile? At least *try* to find something better? We can spare a half an hour."

We drove around for a while. It was hopeless. In Iowa at one in the morning it is hard to find a light on anywhere, even in the distance, much less a charming cabin in which to shtup. We found ourselves on a narrow side road. I told her she was being emotional.

"Turn in here!" she said suddenly.

There were two ruts wandering into a cornfield. I slowed to a crawl. It was bumpy, designed for a tractor.

"This is far enough," she said.

I stopped. She snuggled up to me and kissed me on the cheek. Well, okay, she wanted to neck, to work up her nerve. I turned everything off. Maybe I could get her so inflamed she would go wild and *beg* me to take her to the Riverside Motel. Maybe I could register by phone and have her crouch on the floor while I shot through the arch at fifty miles an hour.

I had never known her to be so affectionate. She was covering my face with kisses and caressing my head and neck. I nearly fainted when she took my hands and moved them to her breasts . . . that was not like her at all. With her mouth glued to my mouth her hands left me and she writhed mysteriously. She pressed a ball of silky cloth into my palm.

"What's this?"

"My panties."

"Your panties? The ones you were wearing?"

"We're going to do it right here."

She started unbuttoning her blouse.

"You want to do it in the car? Instead of the motel?"

"I'm not going to that motel, so forget it."

I took off a shoe. "Can it be done in a car?"

"Love will find a way."

I can remember watching her undress in the starlight, but I don't remember undressing myself. I remember the two of us naked, embracing, trying to avoid the steering wheel and the gearshift handle, which rose out of the floor at exactly the wrong spot. Once we honked the horn by accident, and once we bumped the shift into neutral, allowing the car to lurch several feet alarmingly.

In the front seat it was impossible, so we clambered over the top into the back, a tangle of arms and legs and breasts and hair and knees. With more room to maneuver we had no trouble working each other into a frenzy. When everything was ready, I broke open the packet and removed the prophylactic. It was a membrane stretched over a circular rim the size of a half dollar. The idea was to roll it onto your swollen member the way a woman rolls hosiery onto her legs. No one had explained that to me. Like a fool I unrolled it first and tried to pull it on all at once the way I would a galosh. It wouldn't work. After an inch or two the thin latex adhered to my skin and wouldn't advance. I wondered if Wayne had given me an extra small size as a ghastly joke.

"What's the matter?"

"I can't get the goddam rubber on. Look the other way, I'm going to turn on the overhead."

There was no bulb in the tiny socket. I struck a match. In the brief flare of yellow flame I was able to examine myself. I saw the Eiffel Tower with a sagging wind sock on top. With my free hand I tugged at the rim of the rubber, trying to pull it on another inch or two at least. It wouldn't budge. The flame burned my fingers and went out.

"Aw, shit, it's no use. It's hung up. I think I tore it."

"Don't bother, then. I just had a period . . . it's probably safe. I'll douche when I get home."

That suited me. If she got pregnant her family would have to accept me and she would have to marry me and we

144

would be able to meld and merge every night on a big, flat bed.

We rolled around, trying to find a feasible position. The best we could do was facing each other with our bodies straight, our feet planted on the floor on top of our clothes and our heads against the rear window. By arching our backs we could bring our stomachs together, but there was something wrong with the alignment where it mattered. I made a few compulsive thrusts with my hips but didn't get lucky. I was a caddy trying to replace a pin at a forty-five-degree angle.

Rachel made a regrettable mistake in an effort to be helpful. She decided to use her hand to guide the sword to the sheath. When I felt the fingers I loved close around my manhood, coaxing and tugging, my mind blossomed with erupting volcanoes, gushing spigots, bursting dams, and ruptured hydrants. I had a roller-coaster sensation of all the blood, lymph, and phlegm in my body suddenly being sucked into my penis and shot into the night sky.

"Oh my God!" Rachel gasped, "it's going off in my hand!"

It was going off in her hand!

"It . . . it is?"

She collapsed into a sitting position, still holding on.

"Can't you stop it? Can't you turn it off?"

"I . . . I . . . I . . ."

"Oh! It's getting all over me!"

"Don't point it *this* way!"

She pointed it at the upholstery, then tried to muzzle it with the palm of her other hand. I twisted out of her grip and doubled over in the corner until the spasms subsided. I closed my eyes, gasping. When I looked at Rachel again she was dabbing at her thighs and midsection with my shirt. I helped her, then tried to dry myself and the upholstery. Cursing and groaning, we stood in the weeds outside the car and got dressed. Our clothes were wrinkled and spotted and more or less ruined for anything except gardening.

I tried to apologize but she would have none of it, insisting that it was entirely her fault, that she should have gone through with what we had planned. She told me I had nothing to be embarrassed about, and on the way back to

Ames she kissed me several times on the ear to reassure me. My roommates were wrong about her being selfish. She certainly was considerate of my feelings that night, when a few cheap remarks would have wounded me for life.

Our second plan seemed foolproof. Rachel agreed to visit me on Saturday afternoon in the basement of Mrs. Lurella Parkhurst's bungalow. My roommates, I assured her, were gone for the weekend and would never know a thing about it. Actually they had merely agreed to stay away until nightfall, helping me clean the apartment before they left.

"Yoo-hoo," Rachel called, rapping lightly on the open door. "Anybody home? Avon calling."

I welcomed her with a kiss. She was dressed as if she were applying for an important job. Her reaction to the apartment, to the domination of the decor by the furnace pipes, was one of dismay.

"You *live* here?" she said, walking slowly around, shaking her head, "with *how* many other people?"

She ran her fingers along the backs of our kitchen chairs, and for the first time I noticed how rickety and cheap they were. She glanced at the stove and refrigerator; St. Vincent de Paul would have thrown them out. I was struck by how out-of-place Rachel seemed. Her face had a definite aristocratic cast, and her clothes, I knew, were picked out by her mother at Marshall Field and Neiman-Marcus. With her shoes, her bag, her suit—inappropriate for the time of day and the occasion and obviously expensive—she could have been a politician examining a slum for the benefit of photographers.

"It's so clammy and gloomy down here," she said, "how can you stand it?"

"We keep the lights and stove on. It gets cozy." I turned on the stove to prove it.

She was at my desk, touching my few possessions. "At least you have some good books." She picked up *Man and His Gods* and kissed it. "This one changed my life. I wonder what Homer Smith is like? If he asked to sleep with me I'd let him, out of gratitude."

"He didn't ask you. I asked you."

I embraced her. We looked at each other. Her expression

146

was one of *bravery*. She gave the impression of being determined to go through with the coupling, even though she didn't care for the facilities. She may not have loved me anymore. Alex said that the reason she got interested in me in the first place was that as a small-town Irish Catholic I was, to her, *exotic* . . . a characteristic that would fade with familiarity. It may have been that she wanted to go to bed with me simply to prove that she was independent of her parents. As for myself, I had a hard-on and was uninterested in such nuances.

I locked the door and propped a chair against the knob. She made sure the curtains were fully drawn over the windows, then inspected the bathroom. There was nothing to apologize for in the bathroom: It was nearly new and firstrate in every respect. It was the only thing she commented favorably on all afternoon.

We had already agreed to begin with a ritual shower—an idea that so appealed to her sense of cleanliness, good grooming, and symbolism that it overcame her shyness about daytime nudity.

We undressed each other. When she was naked she blushed. She was exquisite, fawnlike, a goddess.

The shower wasn't quite as much fun as I expected. The stall was too small for comfort. We couldn't find a temperature for the water that fully suited both of us. When the soap dropped it was almost impossible to pick it up without being rude. The most enjoyable part was soaping her. I covered every square inch with suds. Displaying commendable maturity, I lingered only slightly longer than necessary over her breasts, not making a major project of them. I tried to treat her various areas in a fair and equitable manner. To me she was a unified work of art.

The disaster began when she soaped me. Halfway along she straightened up and gave me a look of horror. She turned to the wall. "Oh, *no!*" she said, as if Japan had bombed Pearl Harbor again.

I thought she was going to faint or scream or throw up. "What's wrong? What is it? Are you all right?"

She wouldn't tell me. She looked ill, wouldn't tell me what ghost she had seen, what disease had flared up. She finished soaping me without élan.

We rinsed ourselves and stepped out of the stall. I dried

her with a fluffy towel. She was wooden and desolate. I tried to make her smile by the way I used the towel, but nothing worked. She dried me superficially, finally dropping the towel and wandering out of the bathroom. She stood naked in the kitchen, staring at the hockey stick. I took her by the hand and led her to the bed. I turned down the sheets and blanket. Instead of getting in she sat on the edge, folding her hands in her lap and staring at them. I sat beside her and asked her again to tell me what was wrong.

"Tommy, you didn't . . . you should have . . . I didn't realize . . ."

"What is the matter? *Tell me!*"

She began whimpering. "You're not . . . you're not circumcised!"

"For God's sake, so what? *That's* what you're upset about?"

"Why didn't you tell me? I never *imagined* . . ."

"Didn't you notice in the car? When you grabbed me?"

"It was dark."

"Who gives a damn?"

I put my arm around her and kissed her cheek. She pushed me away.

"Don't. I can't. I couldn't."

"Why the hell not? Goddammit, Rachel, look at me! What difference does it make?"

She couldn't look at me. "I . . . I—I don't want to be . . . be all filled up with . . . all filled up with . . ."

"With what? With what?"

"With *smegma!*" she sobbed openly.

"Smegma! Are you crazy? I don't have any smegma! Did you see any smegma?"

"People with foreskins have it. Underneath. It accumulates."

"I keep myself clean! We just took a shower! Show me the smegma! I defy you to find any smegma! I'll turn on the gooseneck."

She grabbed my arm.

"Please," she said, "I'm not a federal meat inspector. There might be some and I'd miss it. I think it's invisible."

"Invisible smegma? You're out of your fucking mind! So

148

what if you miss it? Since when has a little smegma ever hurt anybody?"

"It causes cancer, that's all."

I rolled my eyes. I couldn't believe what I was hearing. "That's ridiculous! The most ridiculous thing I ever heard in my life, and I was a Catholic! It's some crazy Jewish superstition. Don't you see how crazy it is? How unscientific? Use your *brain!*"

She swallowed and looked at me. She spoke evenly. "I am using my brain. It is not a superstition. It is a matter of scientific fact that Jewish women have less cancer of the uterus than gentile women do. That's not crazy. That is a proven scientific fact. I am amazed that it is news to you. The reason for it is that Jewish men are circumcised."

"What scientist said that's the reason? Even if what you say is true, what proof is there that that's the reason? It could be a lot of things. Maybe Jewish women have built up a resistance to cancer from eating unleavened pork or some goddam thing. Who made the study? Ten to one it was a Jewish scientist."

"I'm not going to debate it. Honestly, I don't see how you can go through life like that." She stood and started dressing. "I don't see how you could even think of making love to me when you are in that condition. I'm shocked."

"There is nothing wrong with my condition! Lots of famous people have my condition! Julian Huxley! George Mikan! Bertrand Russell! Fulton Sheen! Robert G. Ingersoll!"

"You are making that up."

"Rachel, this is just an excuse. You are still afraid of your mother and father."

She whirled on me and shouted, "I don't want to get cancer! I don't want you putting smegma inside me and giving me cancer! I don't want my uterus to fall out! Can't you get that through your thick skull?"

I shouted back, "That is stupid! How can I give *you* cancer if *I* don't have it? If your uterus fell out, then so would my cock!"

"You think that's *good?*"

There was a sharp rapping on the ceiling. It must have been Mrs. Parkhurst. After a thousand appalling conversations had been carried to her ears by the furnace pipes, she was finally hearing one she couldn't stand another second.

"Sorry!" I shouted in an upward direction. I caught Rachel's wrist and pulled her down beside me on the bed. She was wearing her panties and one shoe. "Now, listen," I said, keeping my voice low, "we are going to talk this out like two rational people."

"I'm sorry I raised my voice," she said.

"Me, too."

"Tommy, I don't think I can sleep with you. All my life I've heard my father talk about how dirty gentiles were for not getting circumcised."

"That's a prejudice. He planted that in your mind. It's up to you to reject it. Like all top violinists being Jewish."

"What has that got to do with it?"

"It shows you have certain little prejudices you probably aren't even aware of."

"But it's true! It's a known fact!"

"Maybe it is. My point is that you knew when you told me that the Irish didn't go in for violin playing."

"The *Irish*! I've got nothing against the Irish! I was just bragging a little bit, that's all. I'm proud of what the Jewish people have accomplished in science and art."

"If you made a list of the hundred greatest police chiefs and city street superintendents in the country, I'll bet the overwhelming majority would be Irish."

"You mean I have to sleep with you to prove I don't hate the Irish? Would I be sitting on your bed half naked if I hated the Irish? Haven't I told you that some of my favorite writers and poets are Irish?"

"It's not fair for you to be half naked and me to be stark naked. It puts me at a disadvantage."

She kicked off her shoe and slammed her panties on the floor.

"I'll give you three minutes to state your case, then I'm leaving."

"All I ask is that you reconsider the smegma thing. You are a very bright woman and I know you'll act on the facts rather than on your emotions."

"I'm listening."

"Your father put the idea in your head that foreskins were bad before you were old enough to make up your own mind. You were biased on the subject. When you ran across the medical research report you might have given it more weight than it deserved because it supported a preconceived notion. The study might not have been concerned with people in our age group or nationality. The sample may have been too small. The differences alleged might not be statistically significant. Even if they were they might not be due to circumcision—they might arise from diet or genes or any number of things. I know something about statistics and permutations and combinations. What's involved here are simultaneous equations with millions of unknowns. They can't be solved with any certainty."

"That might all be true, but I'm still scared."

"I'm not done. Has any Omicron Ep ever said she wouldn't sleep with an uncircumcised man? If he was clean?"

"No. But I've never really taken a poll, either."

"If there were a serious danger, don't you suppose somebody would have mentioned it?"

"I guess so."

"If I called a cab for you after we made love, you could get to a douche bag within minutes, couldn't you?"

"That's crude."

"Finally, there's this. . . ." I held up another one of Wayne's top-grade reservoir-tipped prophylactics. "Even if smegma is as evil as you say it is, this will keep it bottled up."

"I forgot about that thing. Have you figured out how it works?"

"Yes. Rachel, I don't want you to sleep with me to prove you don't hate the Irish or to prove your independence. I want you to sleep with one particular Irishman to prove that you love him, or at least that you don't hate him. I love you, I think. I love you enough to marry you."

"Oh, you don't have to say that! I don't require that of you. Your Catholic upbringing is showing—sex before marriage is a sin and all that. All right, I'll make you a deal. I'll call a cab and tell it to be here in thirty minutes. That'll give us time enough to prove our lack of prejudice. Tomorrow I'll go to the library and research the foreskin thing, see if there is anything to it." A few minutes later she was slipping gracefully under the covers. "Come on," she said, extending her hand. "Once isn't going to kill me."

"You're so romantic."

It was the most wonderful thirty minutes imaginable, and when the cabdriver honked his horn in the driveway I could cheerfully have run outside and strangled him.

22

Terrible News

Just as euphoria was setting in, my father died. It was as if God paused on his way out of my life to commit one last act of vandalism.

The day before I got the news, I was able to put in six solid hours of studying. Losing my virginity had given me the necessary peace of mind and sense of purpose. Getting straight A's now would be no problem. When I closed my sewage texts at dusk, I stared into space with a smile. Sex with Rachel had been glorious and I was yearning for an encore. To believe that our act of love deserved punishment by the fires of hell was monstrous. I felt not the slightest twinge of guilt; I knew too much for that now. After years of torment I had broken through to the truth! Priests and nuns and popes were just ordinary people in obsolete clothes! There is no hell! Morality and good citizenship have nothing to do with religion! On the contrary! I felt like knocking on doors to spread the good news. I definitely would try to convince my relatives and friends in Dubuque that I was right and they were wrong. "Take off your blinders," I would tell them. I imagined myself standing before a spellbound audience that included Sisters Raphael, Conceptus, and Don Bosco; Fathers Grundy, Slattery, and Breen; and my parents, and turning their weltanschauungs upside down. Man created God in his own image, I would tell them. The Catholic Church is a pastiche of magic and paganism. Life after death is wishful thinking. The Bible is merely a collection of tribal papers that shows plain signs of editorial tampering. Sex is good. Sin is sick. The only possible way to approximate truth in any field is through the scientific method. The power and clarity of my arguments would lead the priests to tear off their collars and say, "How could we have been so stupid?" The nuns would weep at the realization that they were wedded to a myth. My loving parents would embrace me and say, "Thank you, son, for the gift of intellectual freedom that will enable us to spend our declining years unfettered by absurd superstitions." I saw myself invading Paul's monastery and using my silver tongue to cause mass defections among the latent homosexuals, masochists, social cripples, ex-convicts, and sissies. And if everybody refused to see the light? That was okay, too. I would be perfectly happy hanging around with the likes of Voltaire, Tom Paine, Robert G. Ingersoll, Einstein, Homer Smith, Bertrand Russell, Rachel Isaacs, and H. L. Mencken. I had just discovered Mencken, who once observed: "If the average Christian put his beliefs in the form of an affidavit, it would make even the Pope laugh." I wished I had said that.

Now that I knew all the answers, I could hardly wait to get home for summer vacation and start my missionary work among the believers.

On the day I got the terrible news, I had lunch with Dr. Kellman in his ivied redoubt. He welcomed the chance to invade the student-faculty senate meeting and demand that I be retained as a student. He jotted down a few notes while I tested a string of liver-pâté sandwiches. Later, running for a class, I spotted Rachel across a greensward. We waved, and she shouted shamelessly that she was on her way to the library to research smegma. When I got back to the bungalow and descended the cellar stairs into the gloom, an uncomfortable Alex Gold told me my father was dead.

It was a total shock. Dad was rarely sick, much less seriously sick. When I saw him last he had the flu, but he and Mom both assured me he was getting over it. I stared at Alex in disbelief, wondering if he were attempting a particularly tasteless joke. His frown and his inability to meet my eyes made it plain he wasn't kidding. I walked into the kitchen like a zombie. The books I was carrying slipped out of my hands. At some point I started crying, and I kept crying all the way to the bus depot. Alex talked to me, but I don't remember what he said. I remember that he put his arm around my shoulder and squeezed hard, which was the first time anybody my own age had ever done that.

The six-hour bus trip seemed like six days. I spent the whole time gazing dully at the passing Siberian landscape. I hadn't been a very good son, at least not lately. I had never thanked my father properly for all he had done for me, and now I would never get the chance. I had never told him I loved him. Men in Dubuque didn't normally say they loved each other. A hearty handshake was about as far as you could go, but that was no excuse. I had let my father down. He had sent me to college at great expense and I hadn't even shown the common decency to study what I was supposed to study. Worse, I let myself get so wrapped up in my own concerns that I sent a letter home poking fun at his religion while he was sick. All that stuff about lightning rods and tidal waves! Who the hell did I think I was, anyway? If only I had kept my big mouth shut until he was back on his feet. If only I hadn't told Carolyn I had left the Church. The letter worried me. Could it have contributed to his death? If he had been on some sort of medical fence, able to fall either way, a shocking letter could have toppled him into his grave. I thought he had the flu!

Leonard E. Shannon died of heart failure. The doctor was giving him iron for his blood and Lapactic pills for his bowels while his heart was slowing to a stop unnoticed. The details were given to me by an apparition who met me at the Dubuque bus depot dressed in a burlap tube tied at the waist with a tasseled curtain-pull. On top of his head was a self-inflicted bald spot, and around his mouth was a half-hearted moustache. This eerie man, I was to learn, slept only in hard chairs to emulate his namesake, a fourth-century saint who spent his nights on rocks.

"I am Pachomius," he said.

"Paul? Is it really you?"

"I was once called Paul. Now I am Brother Pachomius. I will drive you home and tell you of the end."

I gaped at him. This lugubrious, malnourished wraith

was "Happy" Shannon, the jolly hero of my youth? We were in the family car and he had forgotten a great deal about driving. I hung on to the edge of the seat and stepped on imaginary brakes as we meandered up Dodge Street, dividing the river of oncoming traffic like the prow of a ship. Pachomius obviously had no doubt that there was a God and that He would protect His troubled children.

Dad had sunk steadily for a week, he told me. One night while reading the *The Saturday Evening Post* he complained of dimming vision and a pain in his chest. Mom put down her iron and filled the hot water bottle. Soon he said he could see only the overhead light. The pain grew. Frightened, Mom called the doctor and began a rosary. Dad's responses grew weaker and weaker. He slipped away during the seventh Hail Mary.

"God blessed him with a beautiful death," Paul said, "as a reward for a life devoted to family and God."

He devoted quite a bit of life to the American Legion and Arnold Gertz, too. I was glad Dad hadn't suffered much, but if he was being rewarded it must have been for something other than to devotion to God. He wasn't particularly religious. Mom had to remind him to make his Easter duty. It crossed my mind to ask Paul why God hadn't rewarded the five choir boys who had died painful deaths a month earlier in Zanesville, Ohio, when their loft collapsed. I let it pass. I had looked forward to engaging Paul in fiery debates, now what I wanted to do was bury my face in his chest and cry the way I had when he came back from the war. By the look of him I could tell that the last thing he needed was an attack from his little brother. We had both lost a father. Now was a time for sticking together.

A few minutes with my mother and I knew that in some sense we had lost her as well. Her mind was no longer centered on its foundation.

23

Funeral Notes

Mom was standing on the porch waiting for us when we arrived. She looked terrible. As I mounted the steps she pointed at me and her mouth began to tremble—I had the sickening fear that she was going to accuse me of murder. Before she could speak she burst into tears and threw her arms around me, told me how glad she was to see me, what a strain she was under, how she wouldn't have been able to go on if I hadn't come home, how she needed both her sons with her to make it through the wake and funeral.

"I'm so sorry, Mom," I sobbed. "I didn't know he had heart trouble. I thought he—"

"I knew! I knew he had heart trouble. It was the doctor who didn't know. I told him he was making a terrible mistake treating his blood and his bowels."

"He wouldn't listen?"

"He said 'Sure' and who was the doctor, him or me?"

"If I had known how sick he was I never would have sent that letter. I hope you didn't let him—"

"The letter! Oh, God, you can imagine what that did to him in his condition! Watching him read it was like seeing somebody take a mop and drive it through his forehead."

"Did you have to show it to him?"

"Of *course* I didn't show it to him. And kill him?"

"I thought you said . . ."

"I burned it the minute I read it."

"So he *didn't* see it."

"He didn't have to."

"You told him about it?"

"No! You can think that about your own mother?"

"How did he find out?"

"He didn't. I kept it from him. The man was dying. What good would it have done?"

"He didn't know?"

"That he was dying?"

"About the *letter*! He didn't know about the letter?"

"He knew! He knew!"

"*How* did he know?"

"He had a *way* of knowing. I could tell by his eyes that he knew. A wise man, your father was."

I looked pleadingly over her shoulder to Paul, who raised a finger and made small circles next to his head. I put my arms around my mother and hung on tight.

"He was a strong man, Tommy," she said, breathing raggedly. "He could have taken your letter in stride, ugly as it was. Don't ever blame yourself for his death. I'm the one it would have killed. I'll always be grateful to him for burning it before I could read it. I found him in the middle of the night in the basement, throwing it into the furnace. I can see him as plain as if we were in a nightmare. Up in flames it went; then I led him back to bed. He never told me what it was. When I found it in the mailbox the next morning, the milkman and I wailed like babies. I couldn't believe my own son was saying such things. Here, take it . . . I never want to see it again."

She thrust a sheet of paper into my hand. It was my letter, looking as if it had been crumpled and smoothed a thousand times.

"I thought you burned it," I said, crying now for my mother instead of my father.

"And not have anybody believe me?"

"But you *said* you burned it."

"I'm not at that stage yet where I'd burn a letter from my own son. I know you'll settle down and come back to the Church when you realize what you've lost. You've always been a good boy."

"Oh, Mom, Mom . . ." Maybe I should have sacrificed

my principles then and told her I was going to communion three times a day, but I couldn't bring myself to do it.

She embraced me again. She said she was glad to see me and not to pay any attention to what she was saying as it was just a manner of speaking and she didn't mean anything by it and had I ever gotten the hard-boiled eggs she put in my laundry.

Brother Pachomius shook his head and made the sign of the cross.

We went inside. The house was full of people. Aunts and uncles and friends and neighbors were in every room. The house was also full of food. Nobody came empty-handed, and a continuous banquet was under way. In the five days I spent at home there were never fewer than six people sitting at our dining-room table, feeding themselves. It was a good thing everybody brought food, because a tremendous amount was needed to take care of the crowd. The commotion was no doubt good for Mom. There was so much chatter, cooking, and dishwashing going on she was never given a chance to feel lonely. Left by herself, she might have gone over the edge. As it was, according to Doctor O'Shea, she had a chance of getting back almost to normal in a month or two. Paul had been given a leave of absence to stay with her at least that long. Every hour or so, when our eyes met across the room, she raised a trembling finger in my direction and seemed about to make some sort of dreadful accusation. Always she stopped herself before speaking.

Except for the food, the scene at the Wilcox and Ryan Funeral Home was the same: a milling crowd of sympathizers constantly being eroded by departures and fed by arrivals. There were many hellos and jokes among those who hadn't seen each other for months, and at times the atmosphere seemed more appropriate for a wedding reception than a wake. I don't know if the festive air was calculated or not, but it had its advantages. It was hard for the bereaved to feel sorry for themselves when everybody was having such a good time. Say what you want about Catholics, they know how to orchestrate grief. I couldn't imagine the Iowa State Free Thought Club having anything to match it.

159

My father's body was laid out in an expensive-looking coffin in a corner surrounded by floral displays, many of them, I discovered from the tags, from barber-supply houses. I lowered myself to a kneeler, hating myself for being unable to resist my curiosity. I would have preferred remembering him at his best; now for the rest of my life I would carry an image of him at his worst. He had lost quite a bit of weight before the end, judging from the looseness of his collar. His hands were folded on his chest, a rosary entwined in his fingers, which struck me as incongruous. I had seldom seen him holding a rosary. A scissors and comb would have made more sense. His color was wrong. Somebody had trimmed the hairs that usually protruded from his nostrils. He was an unreasonable facsimile.

A nun knelt down next to me, crossing herself and smiling. "Don't you think he looks nice?" she said.

"No." I mumbled.

"So peaceful and lifelike."

"It's all over for him, that's how I look at it. The end of the road." I resisted an urge to tell her that wakes are barbaric.

She beamed at me. "Thought of as a new beginning, death isn't sad at all," she said.

"Swinburne wrote a poem about it I wish I could remember, about how death is the end of the line and a good thing, too."

"A new beginning with God."

"Even the liveliest rivers come to rest in the sea, something like that. I'll tell you one thing, nobody is ever going to drain my blood and set me up like a trophy."

"Now he can intercede for us in heaven."

I felt a sudden rush of anger at her obtuseness, and I turned toward her sharply, half hoping I would cause a scandal by shouting at her and half hoping I wouldn't. I had never seen the woman before in my life. In her face was such a look of goodness and sincerity that I choked up and couldn't speak. She didn't have to come to my father's wake, but there she was. By her remarks she was trying to make me feel better, even though we had never met. When I looked into that guileless, shining face, my heart turned to mush. Instead of snapping at her, I embraced her with such vigor that I nearly dislodged her starched headpiece and knocked her off the kneeler. I had never embraced a nun before, and I regained possession of my senses as we struggled to our feet. She patted my back reassuringly and whispered that I had to be strong, not just for myself but as an example to my mother. The time for crying was past, she said. Viewed the right way, as a reunion of a soul with its maker, this was in fact a joyous occasion. Her philosophy may not have been founded on provable facts, but she had a thing or two to teach me about keeping a firm hand on the tiller.

She was the only nun I hugged, not because a lot of them didn't deserve it for coming to the wake and for laboring over me for so many years in the classrooms of St. Procopius, but because there were so many. They filed in by the score, like penguins across the Ross Ice Shelf. I had no idea that the town's cloisters were so densely populated, nor that they would be turned inside out like socks for my father. Sister Raphael was there, and when she reached toward me with a comforting hand I winced, thinking she was going to slap me as a reflex. Sisters Conceptus and Don Bosco paid their respects, their Mount Rushmore faces softened by sympathy. I would have hugged Sister Mary Jean—I liked her more than any other—but she got to me first, embracing me and trapping my arms at my side. Several real tears ran down her cheeks. You can't fake that.

It was amazing how many people came to the wake. I counted nine hundred signatures in the guest book. Nine hundred people over the course of two days! From morning to night the parlors of the funeral home were packed, and the front lawn as well. It was like the county fair without the carnival rides. Arnold Gertz showed up with booze on his breath and talcum on his nose. I was afraid Mom would rail at him, but no; they sat on a bench and held hands for ten minutes, looking straight ahead and not saying a word. They had each lost the most important man in their lives. Porky Schornhorst came in his Marine dress uniform and stood stiffly here and there, looking out of place. He spoke only one word to me. On the way out he nodded curtly and said, "Tough." I had a nice talk with Ellen Ettelsly, who was a postulant somewhere. She was as thin as Helene Hanson was fat. The rest of Helene's body had caught up with her breasts and now she was globular everywhere. There was a time in my lost youth when I couldn't look at her without committing the sin of lust; now here she was looking like Kate Smith. She gave the impression of having become what nature had intended from the start: fat.

So many people! Everybody I had ever known or heard about! The people who played a role in ninety-nine percent of all my memories. Even though I no longer believed everything they seemed to, I desperately wanted to remain a part of their network of solace and support. I no longer had even the slightest interest in standing on a chair and pointing out to them the contradictions in the Bible. Bathed in the river of their emotions and friendship, the great intellectual truths I had recently discovered seemed like minutiae.

I kept my back to the deceased and tried to forget he was there. I stayed well away from my mother, too, who most of the time stood at the end of a receiving line for sympathizers. Two or three times she pointed at me. I don't know whether she was thinking of revealing me as the murderer, denouncing me as a backslider and flunker, or what. She never told me, and I didn't ask. It pained me to realize that she would recover her sanity faster in the company of Paul than me.

During the course of the wake I heard two interesting pieces of gossip. One concerned Father Slattery. He had married a nun and was in Arizona, working in a hospital founded by another renegade priest. A priest marrying a nun! That probably wouldn't happen again in a hundred years. Details were still trickling in. The first clue that Father Slattery had done something odious came from Father Grundy, who, on the previous Sunday at Mass, had offered a prayer for the repose of his soul, as if he had died.

The other news item concerned Joline Breitbach, the girl whose corsage and breast I had once briefly fondled next to the Molo Sand and Gravel yard. She had turned out badly, my Aunt Carrie confided when I asked what had happened to her. A year or so ago, Joline had given birth out of wedlock, married the father, a divorced man, then got divorced herself. When Father Grundy called on her to try to get her to mend her ways and come back to the Church, she told him she had no use for religion and would he please mind his own business. The neighbors overheard it. A scandal! And Joline such a pretty thing—smart as a whip, too. My heavens, Aunt Carrie said, I just don't know what gets into the heads of young people nowadays. She is in Cedar Falls at the teachers college, can you imagine? A person like that wanting to teach young children? It shouldn't be allowed. Oh, and the poor mother! Every time I see Mrs. Breitbach, one of my dearest friends, my heart just wants to break in two.

I agreed that it was a shame and a tragedy that a girl as sharp and pretty as Joline had ruined her life, disgracing her family into the bargain.

I slept in my old bedroom, which my mother hadn't touched except for dusting. On the walls were curling glossy photos of my childhood heroes: Paul as basketball captain of the St. Procopius Apostles, Johnny Mize, Whitey Lockman, Doc Blanchard, Bishop Sheen, and Glen Davis. Paul began the nights in a kitchen chair, but by dawn was snoring on the linoleum, arms, legs, and tassels akimbo.

On the morning of the third day everybody suffered through a Requiem High Mass. I could have turned it into a showcase for my apostasy by sitting defiantly in my pew without budging; instead I stood, sat, and knelt with the rest of the congregation, for which I received several heart-wrenching looks of gratitude from my mother. Father Grundy in his oration eulogized my father in terms so general he could have been talking about anybody in the United States.

There was a dreary procession of cars to the cemetery. Leading the way was a black limousine carrying Mom and Paul. Next were Aunt Carrie, Uncle Ed, and I. There were traces of snow on shaded hillsides.

A winch lowered the casket into a grave. Father Grundy tossed in a handful of dirt to symbolize the ashes and dust whence we came and to which we are doomed. Men stood with eyes downcast and hats in hand. Women pressed kerchiefs to their noses while a chilling wind rumpled their dresses. The scene was extremely cheerless. Fortunately the American Legion was unable to play taps from a nearby hilltop because at the last minute the bugler, the aforementioned Arnold Gertz, called in sick.

Fifty mourners returned to our house for lunch. Not

feeling sociable, I sat on the front steps and watched cars go by. I had lost my father. To a degree I had lost my mother and brother. To those who would say I had lost my soul as well I would argue that I never had one in the first place. It was possible that I no longer had Rachel. The Iowa State librarian might have produced documents proving that smegma was an even worse threat to the public weal than the corn borer. For all I knew, she might have run off with a Jewish violinist.

I looked at the budding trees, particularly at a box elder that had always been a favorite of mine. I had a notion to climb to the top and stay there, advising those who tried to coax me down to go make love to themselves.

24

The View from Square One

On the other hand, things weren't all bad. I had escaped from theological confusion, thus clearing up my asthma. The armed forces, thinking I was a wheezer, had lost interest in me. I had achieved the loss of my virginity, which was worth waiting for. A superior woman had said she thought she might love me and had given herself to me despite her better judgment. Not bad for somebody who still couldn't buy a drink legally. Some people lived long lives without blessings like those.

The mailman came and said he was sorry to hear about my father, who had cut his hair since he was a baby. Probably a lie. I thanked him insincerely. If everybody had patronized my father's shop as they now claimed, he would have been able to build a chain of tonsorial salons stretching from Dubuque to Tierra del Fuego. In the handful of mail he gave me was a letter from Iowa State addressed to my parents. I opened it. It was a carbon of a message that no doubt was waiting for me in Ames.

From: Eligibility Committee
      Student-Faculty Senate

To: Mr. Thomas Shannon
    3rd. yr. Wh. Eng. Cath.

Dear Mr. Shannon:

Based on a strong recommendation from your faculty adviser, a ruling has been made in your favor regarding your application for Spring Quarter probationary status.

Congratulations.

To fulfill the requirements for graduation a year from this coming June, it will be necessary for you to raise your grade-point average to 2.00 or above and to repeat in the next Winter Quarter the course you failed. To make room on your schedule for this repeat, your department recommends enrollment in the Summer Quarter, when both *Solid Waste Compaction* and *Sluices, Flumes, and Catch Basins* will be offered.

Questions regarding your eligibility should be directed to Room 9, Building H, between the hours of 9:00 A.M. and 4:00 P.M.

Closed Saturdays.

Good old Doc Kellman! I made a note to thank him as soon as I got back, maybe give him a gift of some kind. One of those assortments of cheeses and lunch meats might be nice.

Now Rachel began to worry me. I thought she might call and ask how things were going, but there had been no word from her. Was it all over between us already? I didn't see how I could work hard every weekend during the spring quarter without somebody to commit mortal sins with on weekends. Had her father, the corrugated cardboard-enclosure king, permanently soured her against intimacies with the foreskinned? Maybe her family had found about us and secretly sent her to Switzerland to finish her education as a numbered student. What could I do about it? Go to Kansas City and confront her father in the middle of some weird temple ceremony? I couldn't be expected to fight the whole Jewish nation. Rachel wasn't perfect, anyway. Maybe I'd be better off with a girl who was rejecting the same religion I was. Marriage was difficult enough without a spouse who had left a different faith entirely. All my life I had been warned against mixed marriages.

I got up and went inside to make a phone call. I needed some insurance. If I was going to get kicked out of one nest, I wanted another to fall into. I was maturing so fast I could hardly believe it. Only twenty-one years old and already I realized that the woman I loved was not perfect and that possibly she was not the only woman in the world that I could love and be happy with.

"Hello?"

"Is this Joline? Joline Breitbach?"

"Breitbach was my maiden name. Who is this?"

"Tommy Shannon."

"Tommy Shannon? From Dubuque? Well, for golly sakes! Are you here in Cedar Falls?"

"No, I'm in Dubuque for a few days. Got your number from your mother." No reason to mention the funeral.

"You sound different . . . not the Tommy Shannon I used to know."

"I'm older and wiser."

"Aren't we all! Older, anyway. Well, my gosh! What's new with you?"

"Oh, nothing much. I heard some people talking about you, so I thought I'd give you a call and say hello."

"Talking about me? I can imagine what they said. Last time I was there I insulted everybody in sight."

"What I heard was music to my ears."

After a pause she said, "Did you know I was divorced?"

"Yes."

"That I had a baby?"

"I can hear her in the background."

"That I left the Church?"

"Yes."

"Then why are you calling?"

"Because I've swung around to your position myself."

"You have a baby?"

"No, I've left the Church. I want to say I admire your courage and wish you the best of luck. I know how hard it is when you have a lot of relatives and friends that you like."

"It's harder for them than for me. I embarrass them or something. That's why I don't go back to Dubuque much anymore. I'm waiting for the place to loosen up a little."

"I'm an atheist now, I think."

"Come again?"

"I said I'm an atheist now, even though I know there is a logical problem involved. Technically you shouldn't say you are an atheist because you can't prove a negative. I can't prove there isn't a marmalade factory on Mars and I can't prove there is no God."

"What a strange thing to say on long distance."

"I want you to know where I stand."

"I don't know what to call myself. An unbeliever, I guess. Studying and taking care of a kid doesn't give me much time to think about it. After I get my degree, then I'll worry about labels."

"Good idea. You can get all wrapped up in such things and let your grades suffer."

"I suppose that could happen. You're at Iowa State, I heard. Studying what?"

"Studying engineering and trying to get used to my new weltanschauung."

"Your *what*? Did you say weltanschauung? You mean outlook?"

"Yes. You know the word?"

"Sure, but why don't you just say outlook?" She laughed.

There was silence on the line. I couldn't think of any reason why I didn't just say outlook. She had a fine, incisive mind that cut right to the heart of things, eschewing the peripheral. I liked that in a woman.

"Say, Joline, how's your social life? I don't imagine a girl with your brains and looks has much trouble in that department."

"I get by, but the kid is kind of an albatross."

"I'm glad to hear that."

"What?"

"I said I'm sorry to hear that. If I'm ever passing through Cedar Falls I'll give you a call."

"Do that. Listen, the baby is getting into the ink."

"Have you read *Man and His Gods* by a kidney doctor named Homer W. Smith? It's terrific."

"Tommy, I've got to go. Call me again sometime. Good-bye. . . ."

"Good-bye."

I hung up. I went out to the front steps, trying to decide if the conversation had been a success and if I really wanted it to be. Joline was sexy, but she had a kid. Did I want to marry a whole *family*?

Materializing at my side and looking as though he hadn't slept well for years was Brother Pachomius. I was beginning to have trouble thinking of him as Paul. He wanted to have a few words with me about my faith. People were still coming and going and trying to cheer us up, so we sat in the Chevrolet as if we were planning to knock over a gas station.

Pachomius said he was empowered to hear confessions and that if I wanted to straighten myself out, wipe the slate clean, and wash myself in the blood of the lamb, I could do it right there, right there in the Chevrolet. I said I didn't have the slightest intention of doing any of those things, and he said he couldn't see how anybody in his right mind could feel that way, and I said it might be fecund to dig into who was in his right mind and who was not. He asked me if I was denying that God commissioned the Catholic Church through Jesus Christ to deal with various matters and if I thought the universe had gotten here by accident, and I said that that was exactly what I was denying and that there was no way of comprehending how the universe got here. I told him about the earthquake in Lisbon in 1755 and the explosion in the church basement in 1769 and the two criminals in a dungeon who were the only survivors when a volcano wiped out forty thousand people on the Catholic island of Martinique in 1902. He looked at me with such sorrow that I was reminded of Mom and of Christ on the cross. A large trembling tear appeared in his eye when I reminded him that religions had supported every corrupt government down through the ages, that the emperor Constantine had put Catholicism in the driver's seat through the use of the sword, and that many of the early popes were crooks. For weeks I had rehearsed the arguments I would use. I expected Paul to rant and rave and try to dominate me the way he had when I was in eighth grade and he was a hero home from the war. I think I secretly hoped he would hit me with a blitz of facts in opposition to mine that would force me to reexamine my position. Instead he ignored facts altogether. He looked at me as if I were a loved one on a deathbed. He had the decency not to say that Dad had died of a broken heart, but he did say that I was breaking Mom's, and that unless I made a full confession I couldn't be buried in the family plot. He spoke with quiet conviction, and the weight of two thousand years of history was behind his words.

I started to tell him about Eufane Macalyane, who was burned alive in Scotland in 1591 for using an anaesthetic during childbirth, but my voice trailed off. It was obvious that my words were chosen in advance and rehearsed. I was just as bad as Father Breen, the Irish retreat master, which is not to say we both didn't believe our lines.

"I'm sorry, Paul," I said, "I didn't mean to make a speech. I don't want to argue with you. On the way to Dubuque I did. I was going to show you that my way of looking at things was right and yours was wrong. What's the use? We both think we're right, and arguing won't help." I lowered my forehead to my hand. "It's been rough the last few months. I got lousy grades. I had trouble with a girl. Now Dad's dead and Mom isn't right." When I felt his hand on my arm I looked up. For a moment I saw him as he used to be, with fuller cheeks, clean-shaven, and in a St. Procopius letter sweater. "There were a lot of times I would have phoned you to talk things over," I said, "but you've changed so much I hardly know you. I figured you didn't have a phone, anyway. Do monks have phones? Aw, jeez, Paul, do you have to be a monk? You never smile anymore. You used to be my hero."

He stared at me without changing his expression. "There are many happy people in my order. I . . . I'm having my own problems. I wish you had tried to call. You are hard to recognize now yourself. Did you know that? Even though you look the same. Something mean is showing through that wasn't there before."

Aunt Carrie rapped on the windshield with a spoon. There was a long distance call for me. My brother opened his door and started to get out of the car. He said I was a more serious case than he had been led to believe. I grabbed him by the cincture and held him back. In a trembling voice I told him I couldn't believe things just because he wanted me to. Belief wasn't something you could will into existence. I told him I simply wasn't the believing type and that he would have to accept that. He threatened to mail me some books to read, and I said if he did that I'd mail *him* some books to read. We finally agreed to leave the post office out of it. He said he would pray for me. I said I didn't believe in prayer but that I wished him the best. I also said that I had seen a lot of monks, priests, and nuns who looked healthy and happy and that he looked neither and should think about seeing a psychological counselor and he said I should think about the same thing. I let him go. He hobbled away on his false foot, looking ninety-five years old. I wished there was a God I could ask to help him.

The phone call was from Rachel.

"Rachel! Oh, Jesus, it's good to hear your voice!"

"I didn't know if I should call. I don't want to intrude."

"Hang on a second. . . ." I took the phone into the hall closet and shut the door behind me. Wedged among the coats in the darkness, I had a measure of privacy.

"How are things going?" Rachel asked.

"Not so hot. I'm going to miss my Dad. Mom can't look at me without breaking down, and her mind has slipped. My brother the monk looks so bad and acts so strange I can hardly believe it *is* my brother. I just had a long, frustrating argument with him, so things are really swell. I've been crying a lot. I've cried more in the last four days than in the whole rest of my life. My eyes feel like two raw onions."

"I'm terribly sorry, Tommy. I miss you."

"You do? That's good news. I miss you, too. I think of you every couple of minutes. There's other good news, too. Doc Kellman swung it with the senate, so I'll be able to stay in school."

"Wonderful! That should help cheer you up. I have something else that should help, too."

"Yeah? Tell me. I need it."

"It's about circumcision. I found out that Jewish women do have slightly less cervical cancer than average, but mainly in Central Europe. There's no evidence at all to show that no foreskin is better than a clean foreskin."

"Thank God for that!"

"All you have to do is keep it clean."

"I do. Twice a week I used steel wool and a whisk broom."

"Did you know that Egyptian mummies are circumcised?"

"No."

"It's true. And there's an English doctor who thinks that circumcision does more harm than good. He says the reason it got started in the desert countries was because of the way sand tends to work its way under everything. Isn't that interesting? I can hardly wait to argue about it with my father."

It was indeed interesting. It suggested that Rachel and I could express our affection without calling a cab. The next day I was packed and ready to go back to school.

Pachomius gave me a lift to the depot. He told me he felt profoundly sorry for me and that on my deathbed, unless I recanted, I might bawl for a priest and be unheard. He said he would pray for me every day. I wanted to tell him that he was welcome to pray for me, but that I couldn't help feeling his time would be better spent in the garden. I wanted to say that I thought that the reason he seemed so unhappy with life was that deep down in his heart he didn't believe what he was professing to believe, and that on his deathbed he would admit it. I thanked him for his concern for me, and to my everlasting credit I said nothing more.

I bought a ticket and sat on a wastebasket waiting for the bus to Ames, Des Moines, Guthrie Center, Wiota, Fiscus, and Omaha. I didn't sit on a bench because they looked like pews. I thought back to the first time I waited for the same bus. My father was there then, giving me a pep talk. Hit those books, he had said. Get good grades! Show them you mean business right off the bat!

This time I would.

Epilogue

A week after returning to school, I took Rachel to a movie. After we had taken our seats, she whispered, "Do you know what you just did? In the aisle?"

I didn't know what she was talking about. She told me I had genuflected.

"I did not!"

"You did."

"I did not!"

"Tommy, you did. Absentmindedly. A couple of people noticed it and laughed."

She wasn't laughing. She looked concerned.

"It's the second time you've done it since you got back. Yesterday, when we took the bus downtown, you blessed yourself when we passed the state office building."

"Just habit. We were taught as kids to do it when passing a church. If you're not thinking you do it in front of any imposing edifice." I started to sweat.

She pushed ahead relentlessly. "You didn't do it before your father died. Only since."

"The funeral was traumatic. Getting all that affection and sympathy. Seeing my mother and brother and relatives."

She squeezed my hand. "Don't worry. I'm going to help you get over all these things."

I knew what she meant by "all these things." She didn't mean genuflecting and crossing myself. She meant my plumbing failures. For some damned reason, after getting ten thousand erections when I didn't want them, I couldn't get one when I did. It wasn't Rachel's fault. She was so loving and patient it made my eyes water.

A few weeks later, cringing with embarrassment, I went to the student health clinic and told my story to a psychological counselor. He said temporary impotence was perfectly normal in a case like mine. He said I was mourning the loss of my father, the partial loss of my mother and brother, my religion, and the loss of my childhood innocence. He said I was afraid of losing the esteem of the nine hundred loved ones who signed the guest book. He said I was feeling guilty about trying to engage in an act that had been characterized all my life as illegal. One can't expect, he said, to throw off a comprehensive belief system like Catholicism as casually as one does an old sweater, not in view of the psychodynamic cross-currents.

I said I didn't give a hoot about the psycho-dynamic crosscurrents. All I wanted to know was would I ever be able to go all the way again?

Science wasn't able to answer that question with any degree of precision, he said, a little too objectively for my taste. Too many variables. Crucial was the attitude of the woman with whom I was trying to achieve intimacy. She had to be understanding, affectionate, and patient. I had to get used to her and feel sure she wasn't going to flee. Because I had lost the faith of my fathers as well as my father himself, he said, it was not surprising that I was experiencing symptoms of sexual dysfunction. Returning to the Church was not necessarily an answer because I might feel drenched in guilt for having left and for the doubts that would remain.

In other words, it didn't make any difference whether I was in the Church or not. Either way, I couldn't score.

How long would I experience symptoms of sexual dysfunction? I was twenty-one years old. I only had about fifty good years left.

He couldn't say. He did say that even when I could once again achieve intimacy, the dysfunction was liable to return later in life whenever I was feeling tired, drunk, guilty, or nostalgic, which was perfectly normal and nothing to worry about and I should make another appointment on my way out.

It was very discouraging. I couldn't accept the theology

of the Church, but I missed the sense of belonging and security it once provided. I liked the grandeur of its ceremonies and the way it never changed. I didn't want to lose my mother, my brother, and nine hundred loved ones. Building a new and balanced weltanschauung for myself was going to be harder than I thought. I could see myself having to come back to the clinic four, five, even six more times.

I walked home in a daze, wondering why such big-shot freethinkers like Voltaire, Robert G. Ingersoll, and Clarence Darrow didn't warn me that something like this might happen.

In the following weeks I grew to envy my brother Paul. He knew exactly how he was supposed to act and think at all times. He didn't have to deal with the big questions because they were answered in the Baltimore Catechism. He was comforted by a cloak of faith. Girls weren't a problem because thick, high walls kept them out of monasteries. He didn't have to worry about clothes or food or landladies. He had what I guessed was the profound pleasure of knowing that when he died he would be rewarded in heaven for his sacrifices and good works on earth. His trouble-free days were spent praying for people and working in the garden. Not a bad life. Paul would probably gain weight and cheer up when he got used to it.

I managed to stop worrying about the meaning of life long enough to do some good, hard studying and salvage passing grades in every course. I did so well on the Solid Waste Management final that the professor complimented me personally. He shook my hand and looked at me closely, maybe to make sure I wasn't an imposter. Doing well in that course, in which it looked as though I were headed for a certain F, had a tremendous impact on me. It proved that there wasn't anything wrong with my brain and that college work wasn't too hard for me after all, two fears that had been gnawing at me. The professor's handshake came five weeks after my first visit to the campus psychologist and restored my confidence in myself in some profound sense. That night in the back seat of Archy's car, Rachel and I were unable to find any trace of sexual dysfunction. I canceled the rest of my appointments at the clinic.

In a fantastic stroke of luck, Rachel was just getting over a period, so we were able to check into a Boone motel and spend a weekend violating each other without precautions or restraint. In the space of forty-eight hours we were symbolic no less than nine times, beating my old record by eight. A week later, when I put her on a bus to Kansas City to begin her summer vacation, she confided with a sweet smile that her nipples were still sore from the way I had greedily used them for solace and succor.

And yet, as I waved at the bus pulling out of the Ames Greyhound Depot, I wondered if our affair would survive the summer. Certain problems had begun to appear, problems I hadn't noticed when I was crazed by lust. For one thing I knew she felt that even though both Catholicism and Judaism were false and discredited, Judaism was nevertheless superior. In some way Jews were superior to Catholics, although she never came right out and said that. For another thing she treated me as a kind of emotional and religious cripple in constant need of kindness and support, which she, with her richer cultural background, could provide. That may have been true at the beginning of the spring quarter, but hardly at the end. One of the reasons I was in engineering school was that I wanted to *solve* problems; I didn't want to *be* a problem.

I can't criticize her behavior during the five weeks my reproductive equipment was in drydock. She was as understanding, affectionate, and patient as any doctor would have wanted. But a subtle cooling off following the weekend in the motel made me wonder if she was in fact glad to be getting away from me for a while, or for good. She wasn't cruel, and it may be that she simply was loathe to drop me when I was passing through a flaccid phase. The only argument we had at the time had to do with psychiatrists. She got me to agree that the job psychiatrists did took more brains and skill and sensitivity and training than any other, after which she added as a supposed afterthought that the vast majority of them were Jewish. The same sort of thing all over again.

Things weren't going well at the Free Thought Club, either. I resented the implication that religious people were somehow dumb. My parents, for example, and my aunts and uncles and cousins may not have been college-

176

educated, but they were not dumb. The Shannons, my father often said, were not dumb. It was crazy to suggest that Fulton J. Sheen and Mortimer J. Adler and Thomas Aquinas were dumb. I found myself standing up during meetings and arguing the point. I defended the Church as well. The Church must be providing something that people need, I said, otherwise it wouldn't have lasted so long and have so many members. From personal experience I told them that going to confession made a person feel good. There was obviously something to be said for ritual, I said, although I didn't know quite what. I think Rachel thought my mind was becoming unhinged because of my sexual dysfunction.

On the other hand, my relationship with my mother improved tremendously. She was answering my letters again and sending me religious leaflets and hard-boiled eggs. I talked to her on the phone a couple of times and she sounded completely normal, full of plans for turning the house into two flats, with my bedroom becoming the upstairs bathroom. The first step was to clean the house thoroughly, which was right down her alley. One of her letters brought a lump to my throat:

Dear Tommy,

It is nice of you to apologize for the grief you caused me and Your Father. I know you are young and going through a Stage. You have always been a good boy and would not do it on purpose. The Catholic Church and Father Grundy, who is not one of your favorites, and the nuns have been a great comfort to me since Your Father died and will be there when you need them, too.

I will mail your laundry in the morning. Your shorts looked so raggedy and sad I bought you two new pairs from the insurance money. I'm using them to wrap a jar of peaches I put up last Fall. Tell me if it leaks.

Paul says hello and is a big help.

Always remember that I'm your mother and will stand by you and back you up no matter what kind of trouble you get into with the Church or the Police.

Your Mom

P.S. You can't tell me that people who leave the Church are happier. I pray for you. Don't shut God out.

I went home for the ten days between my last final and the start of the summer quarter. When I got to Dubuque I was in for a big surprise. Paul met my bus. It was definitely Paul and not Pachomius. He wasn't wearing his cowled robe. He was in a pair of corduroy pants, tennis shoes, and a sweat shirt from the Dubuque Parks and Recreation Department. He was clean-shaven and smiling.

"Paul! What happened? Where's your . . . aren't you . . . ?"

"I joined a new outfit, as you can see," he said, shaking my hand warmly. "Is this your only suitcase? Looks like something Dad might have used in the First World War."

"The monastery . . . ?"

"I quit. Well, I didn't quit, exactly. I took a leave of absence. A furlough. They think I'll go back someday, but I know I never will. You look like you've seen a ghost!"

"I can't believe this! I was just getting used to having a monk for a brother."

"We were called brothers, not monks. You had a brother for a brother."

I followed him to the car with my mouth open while he explained his decision. Living at home with Mom had taught him how much he loved the old home town and that he wasn't really cut out for a cloister. He missed sports and girls too much.

"Are you sure you're doing the right thing? I've been doing a lot of thinking lately, and I decided maybe the monastery was a pretty good place for you. You were set for life with nothing to worry about." Christ, now I was trying to talk him *into* being a monk.

"It was too much like the Army," he said, pulling out of the parking lot. His complexion had improved—probably from Mom's cooking—and so had his driving. "I want to make my own decisions. I tried my best to play the part of a holy man, but I never was able to accept it. I never felt comfortable. That's probably why I stopped smiling."

I shook my head. "You fooled me. At the funeral you seemed pretty sure of yourself."

"I did?" He chuckled the way he used to. "You were the one who seemed sure of yourself. You had all the answers."

I looked away and felt myself blushing. "That was two months ago," I said. "I've changed a lot since then."

"Oh? You mean you don't have all the answers anymore?"

"No."

"Good! Glad to hear you're learning something at college."

Mom had my favorite meal ready for me: pork roast with apple sauce and creamed corn, lettuce salad with pieces of bacon and grated carrot in it, chocolate milk, homemade bread and homemade jam. For dessert she whipped up a batch of her dark-chocolate walnut fudge. The smell of it filled the house and made me think of childhood, Christmas, and every happy time in my life. Several times during the meal Mom left her chair to embrace me and kiss me, and for the first time I enjoyed it.

Everybody had a lot to say, and often we were all talking at once. Mom chattered happily about remodeling the house into two flats. She had lost some weight, but looked good and was in high spirits. She made us laugh until tears came to our eyes, telling us about the time Dad had made her try to guess the number of cylinders in a car engine, knowing darn well she didn't have the faintest idea, and how after a lot of frowning she came up with seventeen hundred and forty-six. She should have stuck to guessing beans in jars, at which she was phenomenal. Paul told us how much he liked his job with the Park and Rec and how if Father Slattery kept his promise he would be the next assistant coach at Crown of Thorns. I made Mom cry by telling her that although I would never be a Catholic again in the strict technical sense, I would go to Mass with her while I was home, for old time's sake. I told her, too, that the grades I got from here on out would be so high they would make everybody's head swim.

It was going to be a great year, and I could hardly wait to get on with it.

More Bestselling Fiction from Pinnacle

More
Bestselling Fiction
from Pinnacle